THE GAME MAKER

KITTY THOMAS

THE GAME MAKER

KITTY THOMAS

Burlesque Press

The Game Maker

Copyright 2020 © Kitty Thomas

All rights reserved.

ACKNOWLEDGMENTS

Thank you to the following people for their help with The Game Maker:

Cathy R. Editing
Michelle A. beta reading
Robin Ludwig Design Inc. Cover design and swag
(bookmarks/magnets)
Shirl Rae audiobook narration

1

The phone in my pocket has stopped ringing by the time I manage to unlock the door and stumble into my apartment, kicking the door shut behind me. In my arms are my last bags of groceries. I sit them on the floor and dig out my phone.

One new voicemail.

I recognize the number of the missed call. It's Carolyn, my landlady. A pile of eviction notices in an array of neon colors is stacked neatly on my kitchen countertop. I should have thrown them away, but I'm a masochist like that.

I press the speakerphone button and dial in to my voicemail where the robotic voice helpfully announces that I have *one. new. message.* I love how each word is its own sentence. I take a deep breath and press one to listen.

"Kate, I need you out of the apartment by the end of the week. I've already got someone who wants to move in. I'm very sorry about your situation, but you have to find other arrangements. I don't want to have you forcibly removed; please don't make me the bad guy here."

I slide to the floor and break down and cry. How did this happen to me? I once heard that nobody ends up truly homeless unless they have a drug problem or a mental illness. Well, let me just say, that is a big fat lie. I have no addictions and am the most put-together person I know. And yet, here I am.

It's hard to explain how someone becomes this isolated. Especially in a city of millions. A few years ago, fresh out of college and mourning the death of my parents —car crash—I decided to move to the city and put my advertising degree to good use. I have a few friends back home, but they're casual acquaintances—not the kind of people I can ask for help.

And here in the city? I'm a workaholic. I was working in an agency with far more men than women. What few friendships I have, again, are shallow and not a *hey, can I crash at your place* sort of situation. And I'm the best goddamned advertising exec in a sixty mile radius. I didn't lose my job because I was irresponsible or bad at it.

I lost my job because of Andrew, my boss. Because I made the mistake of dating him and then breaking up with him. The sex was fucking awful. I would rather be single for the rest of my life than suffer through shitty sex with a man who doesn't know which end of his dick does what. Or where my clit is.

You learn so many useless things in school, but where to find the clit is probably the most useful knowledge many men could gain for practical life use. Followed by how to stroke it, tease it, lick it. Alas, Andrew missed that nonexistent day of class at Shit-you'll-actually-use school.

When he fired me, I told him to go fuck himself, if he could figure out how, and flounced off in a huff. I thought it would be easy with my reputation to find a new job, but Andrew beat me to it. I'm pretty much blacklisted in this city. I thought, no problem, I can move. I have no attachments here. But the economy isn't the greatest, and I can't give Andrew as a reference, so all that hard work and reputation I built? Gone.

And now I'm out of time. Out of savings. I'm going to be out on the street in five days if I don't figure something out.

I wipe my eyes with the back of my hands and struggle to stand. I am not that girl—the one who crumples and cries at every little struggle—the one who needs other people to fix her problems. I will figure something out. But I've tried. I've tried jobs outside of my industry. I've tried jobs that are "beneath me". Nobody is hiring, and the few places that are I'm overqualified for, or the pay is so low I'd still be homeless with the cost of living here.

I put the groceries away, get dressed up in a little black dress, and go out. Even though I only have five more days in this apartment I have to get out. Half an hour later, I find myself sitting at a bar. Such a stereotype. Except I'm sitting at the bar of an extremely nice restaurant. To be honest, I'm surprised they even let me in here. You have to have a reservation, but they do have a bar, and I guess I just looked like I knew where I was going, and nobody stopped me.

I'm not sure why I'm here. Is this some last ditch effort

to somehow land a man who can keep me off the street? Is this the level of pathetic desperation I've reached?

I'm on my third gin and tonic when I spot a woman at the other end of the bar who I am nearly a hundred percent sure is an escort. I don't know why I'm so sure about this, but there's something about her that screams *regularly paid for sex*. Hey, I'm not judging.

An escort.

I roll that thought around in my mind for a moment. It's the one industry I haven't sought work in. But wouldn't it be better than homelessness? I can't get pregnant at least. When I first learned that at sixteen I was devastated. And maybe it's why I've thrown myself so much into my work because I knew children weren't in my future, so I'd better build something else to be proud of.

This escort thought continues to roll around in my mind. I'm not blind to my own attributes. I have long, wavy, naturally blonde-streaked hair. Women pay hundreds of dollars for highlights like these that I have naturally. Blue eyes. Long dancer legs. Pouty lips. Natural, not injections. Not sure about the boobs though. I mean *I* like them. I might be the only woman on the planet who likes her breasts just as they are. I'm a B-cup, which I've always thought was the perfect size. Outside of work, I almost never wear a bra, and they stay where they're supposed to. But lots of men like bigger. Probably most of the men paying for it.

And being an escort is likely to be far worse than being with Andrew because then instead of having bad sex with one person I'd be having it with hundreds. The reality of the fantasy I've just spent the past several minutes exploring loses its luster as quickly as it came on. It's like most fantasies that way. The vast majority of them I would never act out because I know the real thing isn't anything like what's in my head. When it's in my head, I'm the one in control, and my imaginary partners fuck like gods.

I scroll through the depressingly short contact list on my phone. Andrew is still in there. And maybe it's because I've had three pretty strong drinks, but I can't stop myself from pressing the call button.

"Hello," he answers brusquely on the third ring. He has a posh British accent that fools people into thinking he has decency or class.

"Hey, it's me," I say.

"What do you want?"

I don't know how I imagined this conversation would go down, and my head isn't clear enough to navigate it in any kind of intelligent way. I'm aware that I'm making an absolute fool of myself. I know how pathetic this is. There isn't enough alcohol in the world for me to not realize that.

I feel the tears coming, and I can't hold them back. I know I sound weak. I don't think I've ever appeared weak to my former boss, not once until now.

"I didn't have anyone else to call," I say.

"Call about what?" His voice is guarded and threaded with more malice than I expected. Even after firing me and ruining my life, even after two months since the day I walked out of the agency, he's still angry.

"I'm being kicked out of my apartment this week. I can't pay rent. I need..." I trail off.

"I already filled your job," he says.

"O-okay," I whisper. I can't ask him to take me back. It's

just not in me. I can't beg a man I can't stand to take me back. The thought of his hands on me makes the bile rise in my throat, even as I know if I could only get past my pride and beg, I might be sleeping in his extremely nice apartment with all my needs met indefinitely.

He saves me from this groveling.

"I don't have a job at the agency, but you could be my whore."

The cruelty in his tone makes me want to lash out and spew a string of curses at him. But I bite my tongue just in time. Of course I can't be his girlfriend again. Only his whore. Fuck this guy. I want to slit his motherfucking throat so badly I can barely think straight.

"Kate? Are you still there? I will take care of you. I will shelter you and feed you and clothe you and take you out to nice places. And you will service me whenever and however I like in return. Deal?"

The tears are streaming down my face now, and people are starting to stare. I hate this man so much. It wasn't just that he was bad in bed. It's that he's a first-class asshole. He treated me like shit when I was his girlfriend. How much worse will he treat me now? But I truly see no other options, no other escape. My life has fallen apart so fast I have whiplash from it. I remind myself that I don't have to do this forever, just until I can find another way forward.

I glance over at the woman across the bar, contemplating once again trying to get a job as an escort. I mean, I'll be a whore anyway, so what difference does it make? Would it be easier with strangers or with a man I already know is a piece of shit?

The man she's supposed to go with has arrived. It's

clear they've never met before, and he's taking her out of the bar and out of the restaurant. She's got large, perky fake tits, and his eyes are drawn right to them, reconfirming that I could never compete in that industry.

"Kate, tell me where you are, and I will come get you," Andrew says on the other end of the phone.

Defeated, I give him the address and name of the restaurant I'm in.

"I'll be there in thirty minutes," he says. He disconnects the call before I can change my mind.

I have a fourth drink because I'll need a fourth drink for this. Then I step outside into the crisp fall air to wait. But the fourth drink was a mistake. I feel woozy all of a sudden and go down like a pile of bricks.

2

My head is pounding when I regain consciousness. I can't bring myself to open my eyes. I'm lying on a hard surface, which seems weird to me. At first I think I'm lying on the ground outside where I passed out, but there are no city noises. Instead, I hear classical music being piped in from a speaker above me.

And I smell... roses. One of those highly fragrant varieties. I must be at Andrew's place. But why the fuck did he leave me on the ground? It's at this point that I realize I'm naked. Also, Andrew doesn't listen to classical music.

Instinctively, I want to bolt upright and cover myself, but I don't have that kind of reaction time. And it's a real struggle to open my eyes. When I do, I'm momentarily grateful to be in a dimly lit room.

"A-Andrew?" I croak out. I want to scream at him for dumping me on the ground in his apartment, but I can barely choke his name out. I wait for my eyes to adjust.

Everything around me is dark gray, and there's no furniture in this room.

Cell, my mind hisses at me. *I am in a cell.*

I push myself off the ground into a sitting position and wait for my vision to go back to normal so I can get a sense of where I am. Did Andrew put me in here? He's a bigger bastard than I thought. This is when I finally realize I'm not alone.

There's a large, dark figure sitting on the ground against the far wall.

"Andrew, you piece of shit. What are you doing?"

I probably shouldn't speak to the person who rescued me from homelessness this way, but I don't care. He needs to grow the fuck up. I expect him to yell at me or threaten to kick me out, but what I hear instead chills me.

"Who's Andrew?"

This is definitely not Andrew's voice. No accent. Plus it's deeper and more frightening. Suddenly the adrenaline hits me, and I have a sudden burst of speed. I back as far from him as I can until I meet the opposite wall. I shield my breasts from his gaze and shift to a sitting position where he can't see other private parts—even though I know he's already seen everything. And possibly done more. I *was* unconscious after all.

As my vision clears further, it seems that the light in the room gets a little brighter. He's wearing a white T-shirt and jeans, no shoes. His dark hair looks a bit disheveled. He's very attractive. Heart-stoppingly beautiful, actually. It's the kind of unearthly beauty that makes me feel relieved for a moment because I know I'm still passed out. This is a weird dream. I just know it is.

It's not a dream, whispers the same evil internal voice that decided to tell me I was in a cell.

It takes several minutes before my mind is willing to accept what has happened. I don't know if someone put something in my drink or if I was just that drunk. I don't know how long this man stalked me before he took me, but I know I'm looking at the man who kidnapped me.

And now the tears come. It takes every ounce of willpower not to break down into hysterical sobs. This reaction is making a lie out of everything I thought I knew about myself. The strength and control I thought I had in my life. Even up to very recently, I thought I was handling things.

But this is the last straw. It's the last tiny push I needed to find myself in a free fall.

Another dark thought pushes its way into my mind. No one is going to be looking for me. Does the man who took me know that? Andrew sure as shit won't look or file a police report.

My landlady might not realize why I didn't pack my things up first, but as nice as Carolyn is, she'll just be glad she doesn't have to have me forcibly removed. She isn't going to report my disappearance to the police. What disappearance? I've been evicted. I'm not supposed to be there.

There is no reality now but me and my captor. I'm trying desperately not to think about the reasons this man took me. To rape me? To kill me? To torture me? He sure as shit isn't going to let me go when he's done with whatever's on his nefarious agenda. I know you can't appeal to a sociopath, and nobody normal does something like this.

Still, I can't help begging. "P-please don't hurt me."

"I won't," he says.

Huh?

"You can let me go," I say. "I won't say anything."

"I can't let you go. I didn't put you in here."

"What?" For a moment, my confusion overtakes my fear. What does he mean he didn't put me in here? Of course he did. Who the fuck can he blame? The invisible demon perched on his shoulder?

He shakes his head slowly. "I'm in the same boat as you, sweetheart."

I glance back and forth between us. He has clothes on, and they don't look like he's worn them for days. Meanwhile, I'm naked. We are *not* in the same boat.

"I don't believe you," I say. "You're playing with me somehow."

He shrugs. "Believe what you want, but I'm not going to hurt you. You're safe with me."

I know it's some kind of trick. He wants me to trust him so he can turn the tables on me. Sick bastard. But for the moment, he isn't lunging toward me; he isn't getting up from his spot on the ground.

So I take this time to get a better sense of where I am. It's a plain gray cell, not really much to see. And actually there is one thing in here—a large mattress. It actually looks nice, like it recently came out of some upscale mattress warehouse. It isn't dirty or dingy, and it looks like it's comfortable. It's larger than a full-sized, but probably not a king. There are no pillows, sheets, or blankets, though.

The mattress is on the floor next to the guy, like he's

guarding it. Behind him and to one side are heavy long chains bolted into the wall. I look behind me to find there are also heavy chains bolted into the wall behind me. I bite back the urge to scream or cry again. It won't do me any good. I have to try to keep it together.

There's a slot in the wall that looks big enough to pass food through but not much else. And there's a door that looks like it has a lot of security on it. But it's not the only door.

To my right, there's another doorway. There's no actual door on it but, instead, a bamboo beaded curtain that almost reaches the ground. Light streams out from it into the cell, and I realize suddenly that this other room is the only source of light.

"What's in there?" I ask, pointing in the direction of the mystery room.

"Bathroom," he says.

I still don't believe this guy is another innocent victim. He seems way too large and in charge, and strong, to ever be in this kind of situation. But as long as he's going to pretend, I'll pretend with him.

"What's your name?" I ask.

He opens his mouth to speak, and suddenly the music shuts off and a dark, menacing voice enters the room through the speaker.

"No names!" he growls. "You will address him as Master."

That's not Andrew, either.

The man's eyes widen at the same time mine do. He seems both shocked and disgusted by this suggestion from our mysterious captor of what I should call him. But neither of us addresses this. We sit uncomfortably, pretending these words weren't spoken.

But then my co-captive speaks. "Let us out of here, you sick son of a bitch! I will fucking kill you!"

The only response is a chuckle. "Yes, put on a brave show for the girl, but in the end, you will both dance for me, my little monkeys."

There's a part of me that wants to go to the other guy in the cell, as if he can protect me from all of this.

The voice crackles over the speaker again. "I will feed you when you've fucked her."

Suddenly I'm glad I stayed where I am—as far away from the stranger on the other side of the cell as I can get. Not that that makes a real difference.

"Fuck you," the man says. "I'm not going to rape her."

"Okay. Starve then. But she'll starve, too. She's quite a little thing. I bet the hunger will get to her first. So you'll get to watch her die. Enjoy."

It's no longer some great mystery why I'm naked and my co-captive isn't. I'm bait for the evil game of our captor. The music comes back on.

We both sit in stunned silence for a minute, staring up at the speaker in the ceiling, as if expecting the voice to return, but it doesn't.

"I need to use the bathroom," I say to the man in the cell with me. Even though I know he's seen me naked, I don't want to just get up and walk in front of him to the bathroom.

He nods, stands, and turns around. "Tell me when you're in there."

I hesitate for a moment but then get up and cross to the

doorway. When I push back the beaded curtain, I let out a gasp. I expected the bathroom to be just like the cell. Plain gray walls, maybe a metal toilet, a sink, and if we were incredibly lucky, a drain in the floor and a shower head. But this is a *real* bathroom. A *luxury* bathroom. This is the kind of bathroom only the very rich can afford. This room is probably twice the size of the cell, and the cell isn't tiny. I notice there is a speaker in here as well piping in the same classical music.

"Okay," I say to the man in the other room.

I wonder why my co-captive isn't hanging out in here. I don't know what to look at first, but I settle on the roses. There's a large bouquet of white roses in a vase on the marble countertop. The colors of the room are warm gold and cream. There's a giant rain shower that can easily accommodate two people as well as an oversized jacuzzi tub. The actual toilet is at the back of the room in another sort of smaller room. There's no door, just a curtain, but it does allow another layer of privacy.

I feel weirdly comfortable about peeing now because I realize with the distance, the extra enclosed toilet space, and the music, the man in the cell won't hear me. It's such a stupid thing to be concerned with right now, but still, it makes me feel marginally better inside the horror of this situation.

After I use the bathroom and wash my hands, I look through the cabinets. There are soaps and lotions and bath oils and bubble baths. No real help for escape here unless we can somehow MacGyver a bubble bath bomb.

There's a full first aid kit. Bandages of all sizes, medical tape, salves, ointments, Hydrogen peroxide, and alcohol. I find this discovery more than a little disturbing. Why is our captor providing us with this stuff, and what will happen that requires it?

In another cabinet are stacks of neatly folded wash cloths and hand towels and bath mats and giant bath towels. I pull out one of the enormous towels and wrap it around myself then walk back out into the main cell, covered now at least.

"Hey," he says.

"Hey. What do we do now?"

We both know what we're supposed to do now, but of course we aren't going to do that. I'm not sure what he'll do if he gets hungry enough. I move back to the place across the room and gingerly sit back down.

"We wait," he says.

"How long have you been here?"

"A couple of days. I've already looked for escape options. There are none." He points up at the ceiling. "In the corners, do you see those shiny black things?"

I squint. I hadn't noticed them before. "Yes."

"Cameras," he says. "There aren't any in the bathroom, though. Though there are probably listening devices in there."

I allow this piece of information to settle in my brain.

"W-when was the last time you ate?"

He winces at this. "Don't worry. I ate half an hour before he brought you in."

"Have you used the shower or the tub?"

"The shower."

"So he's not going to come in here and hurt us if I..."

The man shakes his head. "He won't come in until I eat.

He drugs the food. So if you want to take a bath or a shower, you'll be safe."

"You won't come in?"

He shakes his head. "I promise."

"Do you think he'll starve us if we don't do what he says?"

He sighs. "Yes."

I look away. I don't know what to say to this. It's not as though it would be any great tragedy to sleep with this beautiful man, but I don't think I can do it with someone else watching. I might feel differently about this when I get hungry enough.

Since I'm in no exact immediate danger, I don't cry again. I feel stupidly safer with this other man here even though I know obviously something bad is going to happen, things we'll both be forced to do together to survive. And in the end, we probably won't anyway.

"I'm going to take a bath,"

He nods. He doesn't turn away this time because I'm covered in a bath towel. It takes a while for the tub to fill up. I put in some raspberry bath oil and take one of the roses from the vase and sprinkle the petals in. I'm trying to feel normal. Inside this bathroom, I can pretend that things are somehow normal.

I sink beneath the steaming hot water and lean back against the rim of the tub, closing my eyes and listening to the classical music.

I stay like this until the water goes cool. But no matter what I do, I can't convince myself that I'm having a normal bath on a normal day.

As I'm getting out of the tub and drying off, it occurs to

me, my co-captive knew about this bathroom. He knew about the towels. He could have covered me so I didn't wake up like that. He would have had to have been unconscious when I was brought in, of course. Maybe he'd woken up just before me and didn't have time. Maybe I was already stirring, and he didn't want to startle me. Or maybe... he liked the view and isn't *that* honorable.

I find myself unsettled by these possibilities as I return to the cell.

Hours pass. I try not to look at him, but I fail. There isn't much to look at or occupy my time. The music is becoming a little obnoxious, and to be honest, I would rather have the silence. It's like Chinese water torture.

I mean sure, it's not *drip drip drip drip drip*. But without the ability to turn the music off, it has that same maddening quality.

Whenever I catch myself looking at my co-captive, he's already looking at me, watching in that silent way he does. Despite our shared situation, I can't help feeling like his prey. How hungry is he? Is he thinking about fucking me to get fed? Is he thinking about how easy it would be to just take me? Is he calculating how quickly his conscience might shut up if he just does what has been asked of him?

"You should try to get some sleep," he finally says. His gaze shifts to the mattress beside him. An invitation?

"I-I'm fine."

"I'd bring the mattress over to you, but it's somehow bolted to the floor. I'd switch places with you, but I need to be facing the door."

The wall he sits against is directly opposite from the door to the outside world. My wall, the one I've been sitting against, is the same wall that door is on. The bathroom door is a third wall to my right and his left.

He moves a few feet over, so that he's more in direct alignment with the door he watches when he isn't watching me, but it isn't nearly enough space. "Come lie down. I won't touch you."

I shake my head and stay where I am.

3

I don't know how much time has passed, but I'm hungry, *really* hungry. I've been drinking water straight out of the bathroom sink, but it doesn't stop the hunger pangs.

He sits across the room, watching me, the same way he watched me when I first woke in the cell. I've slept a few times—on the floor—but I don't think that correlates with how many days I've been here. I think it's only been a couple of days.

I don't know. There's no way to measure time.

We haven't really talked much. I'm not sure what one is supposed to talk about in this situation, and I think both of us are afraid that anything we say will give our captor additional ammunition to use against us.

Even though the mattress is only a few feet from him, he's chosen to sleep on the floor. He refuses to sleep on the mattress if I won't sleep on it, like he can't stand the idea of me sleeping naked on the cold, hard floor and him having some measure of comfort—like it offends his sensibilities somehow to the point that he's willing to be just as uncomfortable as me. And I've continually refused the offer.

Even if he'd move far away, I don't want to sleep on it while he sleeps on the floor, either, and if we both sleep on the mattress, I know what will happen next. It's impossible that with our hunger and that kind of proximity that his hands won't wander over my body, that he won't get on top of me and...

"Come here," he says.

I swallow hard, but I don't move. Has he hit his limit with this? We both know what has to happen. Our captor hasn't spoken to us again. Who knows if he got bored and just decided to leave us here to die? Who knows if we'll get food even if we obey at this late stage?

He doesn't repeat his request, just continues to watch me. After a few minutes, he stands and walks across the cell. This is the first time he's been this close. I flinch when he reaches me.

He ignores my reaction and sits on the ground beside me, but he doesn't make any attempt to touch me. Instead, he sighs and says, "Starvation is a bad way to die."

"I know," I say.

"I don't think you do."

I start to cry. It's the first time I've broken down since those first moments in the cell. Supposedly, if we have sex, we'll get food. And I want food, but then what happens? The longer I can delay this, the longer I delay the next steps in whatever sick game our captor is playing with us.

"You know what has to happen," he says, echoing my exact thought of only minutes ago. "What's the point of letting yourself get sicker and weaker than you need to be? You need your strength. You need to eat."

"You mean *you* need to eat," I say, unable to hide the bitterness seeping into my voice. So the nice guy act is finally ending? The gallant chivalry finally coming to an end. Everyone has a limit. And now I know his.

"I'll be fine," he says. "I'll be fine a lot longer than you will. Are you going to let yourself starve to death?"

I chance a look into his eyes. "What do you think would happen to you if I did?"

He shrugs. "He'd probably take another girl, bring more bait to tempt me. He wants to turn me into a monster and you...or whoever... into a whore. That's my running theory, anyway."

He stands and holds a hand out to me.

"What are you doing?"

"Remember what I said about the cameras and the bathroom?"

I nod.

He's still holding his hand out. I try to ignore it.

"I'm not going to hurt you," he says.

I am *so* hungry. Finally, I take his hand and let him lead me into the bathroom. He guides me to sit on the edge of the tub and turns the shower on. Then he starts to undress. I tense, part of me wanting to run back into the cell.

"We're going to take a shower, you and I," he says calmly. "I won't touch you in any way you don't want. And no one will see."

I know what he's doing. He's trying to make this easier for me. In the end, I'll have to fuck him in the cell in front of the cameras so our sick mystery captor can watch. My co-captive is trying to give us some privacy and the illusion of choice at least to start, at least to let me get used to his body.

"Come on, drop the towel and get in the shower with me."

He steps into the shower and closes the door behind him. I know he won't hurt me. He hasn't yet. I think I'm safe with this man, and there's only one way to get food. I take a few slow deep breaths, wipe the stray tears off my cheeks, and take off the towel.

When I open the door, he pulls me in under the rain shower with him. His mouth moves close to my ear. His words are quiet, almost dwarfed by the sound of the water.

"I don't know if there are listening devices in the bathroom, but if there are, the shower may give us some cover. What's your name?"

I pull back from him and look into his eyes—really look at them. I've avoided his gaze so much in my time here. They're hazel, but they seem far lighter than they are because of his tanned skin and dark hair. He's growing the beginnings of a beard.

"Kate," I finally say.

"Kate. That's a pretty name. I'm Seven."

At first I think I don't hear him right. "Seven? Like the number?"

He chuckles. "Yes, like the number."

"Are you from a big family? Are your siblings all named One through Six?"

"No siblings. Only child. I can be grateful they didn't name me One, I guess."

"Yeah, no kidding."

I like his name though. The strangeness of it makes me feel somehow more comfortable with him. But still I flinch again when he moves a strand of wet hair behind my ear, the touch too intimate. I'm suddenly so aware of just how naked I am with this man I don't know.

"You can touch me, Kate. However you want. I'm yours to explore. I want to make this easy for you because we both know you aren't going to starve yourself. And I really don't want to watch you..." He trails off.

He doesn't want to watch me die. Our captor is right; Seven will make it longer than me. And on a certain level, if we don't do what we've been ordered to do, it makes it look like I'd rather die than fuck this man. And that is definitely not true. His body is a work of art. There is no part of me repulsed by any part of him.

It's just the situation.

Even if he'd survive longer than me, I know he must be hungry. And our captor didn't say I had to consent. He just said Seven had to fuck me. All he had to do was take me in that cell, my will be damned, and we would both be fed— at least if our captor plans to honor his own terms. There's no way to know if we'll really be allowed to eat if Seven fucks me.

Suddenly out of nowhere, I'm sobbing, the weight of everything becoming too much. Seven pulls me against his chest. My first instinct is to pull away, but he's so warm and solid, and the way he cradles my head against him makes me feel stupidly safe in the midst of this nightmare.

"Shhh, Kate. I'm so sorry this is happening to you."

I let him hold me as the warm water rains down over

us. Finally, after several minutes, when I'm able to stop my crying, I pull away from him.

I reach out tentatively and run my hands over his chest, sliding down the smooth rippling muscles of his abs. He's got that gorgeous 'V' that only the most dedicated men can achieve. He's tall, maybe six foot three, and broad, but his muscles aren't bulky like a body builder. They are compact, tightly coiled strength. These are not muscles built for looks; they're built for action. Though they are undeniably beautiful.

There's a sharp intake of breath from him as my finger trails along one side of the line of that 'V', then I drag my tongue long it. His cock rises to attention. He is large and thick and hard. Seven has the most beautiful dick I think I've ever seen in my life.

I experimentally lick one of his nipples before biting gently. He groans at this. I look up at him, and he takes the opportunity to put his hand behind my neck and pull me up and into him for a consuming kiss that ignites a whole swarm of butterflies inside my stomach that shouldn't be there but are.

I expect him to fuck me now, but he doesn't. We just make out in the shower for several minutes like a couple of teenagers who haven't crossed that bridge before. I'm panting when I finally pull away from him. He lets me go, his intense hungry gaze never leaving mine.

"No names outside of the shower," he says. "We don't want to piss him off."

I nod my agreement. For a moment, I wonder if he's going to push for more or take me up against the shower wall, but although I know he wants to, instead, he turns the water off and gets out.

When we go back into the cell, I'm wrapped in a bath towel again, and he's dressed in the clothing he was allowed. I go to my side, and after a moment of hesitation, Seven goes to his. He sits in that way he does, watching me. I'm not sure why I went to the opposite side of the cell after what just happened in the shower. Surely we are beyond this necessary distance now.

The voice finally speaks again, the first time in days. "Were you two in there practicing? Well, come on then, entertain me. I'm sure you're ready to eat by now. A steaming hot meal can be yours for the low, low price of your soul and self-respect."

I can see the muscle tick in Seven's jaw. I know he wants to kill this man.

"This is the last time food will be offered. Fuck now and take the food or starve, and I'll start over with two new toys more willing to play my games. Tell me, Pretty Toy, are you ready to fuck him for your dinner because apparently he's just too noble to take what he wants for the greater good. I guess he would rather you die than watch you cry while he takes you. He's got the wrong priorities if you ask me, so it's up to you to save yourself."

I feel the tears prick at the corners of my eyes as I look down at the ground. What else can I do? I don't want to starve to death in here.

"Yes," I finally whisper.

"Yes, Master," he corrects. "I am your Master, and you will address me properly."

"You son of a bitch!" Seven says.

The voice sighs. "Okay, I can see I'm going to have to get new toys to play with. You two are boring."

"Y-yes, Master," I say quickly.

"Good. I can see our girl is at least ready to play, but is our boy?"

I look up to find Seven glaring malevolent holes into the shiny black camera domes above us. I feel the anger radiating off him, and it scares me even though it isn't aimed at me. Just knowing he has that kind of anger while I'm caged with him activates a survival response where I want to become as small and invisible as possible so he doesn't notice me while in this state.

"Pretty Toy," the voice says, once again addressing me, "I think our boy needs convincing to let you eat. Drop the towel and crawl over to him. When you get there, I want you to beg him to fuck you."

I'm crying again. I truly could have sex with Seven without it unraveling my world, but not with this sinister evil psychopath watching and giving orders, intent on making it the most degrading experience possible. But I'm *so* hungry.

My limbs are trembling as I take off the towel and crawl across the cold, hard floor to Seven. He's looking away from me. I don't blame him.

"Please fuck me," I beg. I want to use his name, but I know this will only get us into trouble so I refrain.

"What did I say three days ago?" the voice says. "You will call him Master. You will address us both as Master."

I think somehow it breaks Seven more to be put in this position being shaped and molded into a monster against his will, baited with the promise of food and survival. And not just his own, mine too.

"Please, Master, fuck me." I can barely get the words out.

The muscle in Seven's jaw tightens again, and his face is still turned away from mine. His hands clench and unclench at his sides. He doesn't make a move toward me. It's as though this decision is much harder for him than it was for me.

"Please, just do what he wants. I don't want to die."

Despite Seven's choice to take me into the shower with him, the enormity of *this* seems almost too much for him.

The voice speaks again. "This isn't fair play. She's willing to play my games. If you aren't, maybe I should come into the cell and fuck her myself. Then she can eat, and you can learn a lesson. How would that be?"

"Don't you dare touch her!" Seven shouts.

There is laughter over the speaker. "I can do whatever I want with her. She's mine. She belongs to me. And I'm generously offering to share her with you, to allow you to have a piece of her. But strictly speaking, we don't really need you. So if you want to starve and leave her all to me, I won't complain."

Seven flinches when I reach out and touch his arm. "Please... just give him what he wants."

"Please, Master," the voice patiently corrects.

"Please, Master," I say.

I swear every time I say that word to Seven I think he will completely lose it. There's a pause. He takes a long, slow breath, then finally, he stands and without a word, peels his T-shirt off. The jeans go next. He isn't wearing underwear.

"Lie down on the mattress," Seven says.

I crawl onto the mattress and lie down. It's even nicer and more comfortable than it seemed just looking at it, and I now regret not taking his offer to sleep here instead of on the hard floor.

My gaze drifts to his impressive erection. Whatever moral issues he may have with this situation, it doesn't affect what his body wants right now. He lies down beside me on the mattress and begins to gently stroke me.

I'm sure the voice will interrupt and stop him. I'm sure the voice wants Seven to be hard and rough and mean about it, but there's no interruption. There's no commentary. The touches start innocent and sweet. He brushes my hair away from my face, and runs his fingertips through it several times. He strokes my cheek, then drags his thumb gently over my lip as he unconsciously licks his own.

His hand trails down my neck. Hands graze down and then back up my arms. Gentle strokes down and back up my legs.

"What a pretty bare cunt. I like it," the voice says over the speaker. I flinch at this.

I don't wax for the visual or tactile pleasure of men. I do it for myself. I like the way clothes feel when they brush against that bare intimate flesh. I like the way it feels when my fingers drift over and play with it.

I had a salon appointment a few days ago. I know I shouldn't have. I couldn't afford it. But the cost of rent was so much higher than the cost of waxing, and I just wanted something normal and routine to make me feel like everything in my world wasn't falling apart. That seems so long ago now. The specter of homelessness that had loomed over me now feels so trivial in light of everything.

Seven's eyes are filled with lust, and I know he agrees with our captor about the lack of hair between my legs.

"We'll have to keep her waxed," the voice says. "When the time comes, do you want to wax her, or should I?"

We both know our captor is just trying to upset us. But it's working. Seven goes back to touching me, determined to block out our seedy voyeur. He rubs soothing gentle circles over my belly, and then those same movements happen again with each breast.

I let out an involuntary gasp as his mouth latches onto my nipple and sucks it into a hard point. The arousal that was lacking from my own body suddenly awakens at his mouth on my breast. Then he moves lower.

"Spread your legs," he says, his voice going more guttural. The command is a command by every under-standing of that word. It's as though he's crossed some imaginary bridge in his mind, and he's now ready to play the role of my owner.

I spread my legs, wordlessly inviting him to touch me, to lick me, to fuck me. I'm starting to care less about the cameras because I'm beginning to *need* Seven inside me. Like Seven, my body doesn't care about the actual situation. It wants what it wants. It's a primal dance with music we may not consciously know, but our bodies know, and they want to play this erotic symphony together.

The more he touches me, the less guilt he seems to feel about touching me, the more he treats me as a lover he has every right to possess.

I arch up against his mouth, my fingers desperately clawing at the mattress for purchase, anything to anchor me and hold me to this plane of existence. I moan as he sucks on my clit. His fingers dig into my hips as he greedily devours me.

"Stop," the voice says.

Seven stops, irritated now by this new command. He doesn't want to stop.

"Pretty Toy, look into his eyes and beg him to let you come."

When I look into Seven's eyes this time, a real shift has occurred inside him. Gone is any hesitation to take me. His body and mind are in accord, and I know he will soon fuck me breathless.

"Master, please let me come."

This time when I say that word, he doesn't flinch. His jaw doesn't clench. The anger doesn't show up. There's only lust. It won't take long for him to love hearing that word come out of my mouth. He already wants to love it. I decide this is better. If he winces or turns away when I call him master, it will only shame me. His acceptance and desire is better.

Seven goes back to work on my pussy, his mouth unrelenting until I come, writhing and moaning and panting, unable to control my erratic need to feel these feelings under the precise control of his tongue.

When the pleasure recedes, and I'm wet and open and soft in his arms, he mounts me. I gasp again as he fills me. I've never been with a man this large before, and even after my orgasm and arousal, it takes a moment for my body to adjust to his size.

He begins to move slowly inside me, until I'm once again arching up into him, my body begging him for more of this dark violation.

"Please, Master," slips out of my mouth before I can stop it, and he drives into me harder.

Pleasure tightens the cords in his throat as he lets out an animalistic sound. I join him again, a second wave of pleasure cresting over me as he grinds against my clit. Then he pulls out of me, gets up off the mattress, and puts his jeans back on.

Now that his lust has been fed, he looks guilty, ashamed. He can't meet my eyes. And I hate that. I feel wrong for this, but I liked who he was a few minutes ago, when he didn't give one flying fuck about the cameras or the situation. When I was something he wanted, something he'd decided to take, and his desire and need to be sheathed inside me was the only reality that existed between us.

A couple of water bottles are tossed in through the slot in the wall, then several minutes later, a plate of the promised steaming hot food. Seven takes it as it comes through the slot and then there is a second plate.

One plate is blue and the other is white. Both plates have the same food. Steak, green beans, and a baked potato with just a little butter. It looks and smells delicious, but we'll both have to eat very slowly to not get sick.

The voice comes out over the speaker. "The food on the blue plate is drugged. I'll leave it to the two of you to decide who gets the drugged food. I think you know which would please me, and I think you know you need to factor pleasing me into all of your decisions from this point onward."

I swallow hard, staring at the food. "If I take the drugged food, you can fight him off if he comes in," I say.

Seven shakes his head. "He means the drugs for me; that means the amount is too high for you. It could endanger your life if you eat it. I'm not going to risk it. You are *not* eating the drugged food."

My lip is trembling. "But if you eat it, he could come in here and..."

His expression goes tight. "I know."

"We could split the food on the white plate," I offer.

"That'll just piss him off, and you need a full meal. Fuck! You eat the food. I won't eat. I'm not going to let him come in here and..."

"You have to eat," I say. "If you die, I'll be here with him by myself. Please don't leave me alone with him."

Seven pushes the white plate toward me. "Eat," he says.

"What if they're both drugged, and he's just playing with us?" If that's the case there's nothing we can do. It's either drugged food or no food.

Seven doesn't reply to this. He just watches me. Finally, I give in and start eating. I still think we should have shared this food. But he's right about it making our captor mad, as though we're trying to cheat at his game.

I've nearly finished eating the food on my plate and drinking the water when Seven finally makes the decision to eat his own. He knows there's no choice. He either eats or he dies.

I can tell it pains him to leave me unprotected while

he's unconscious, but what other choices do we really have?

"Come here," Seven says when he's finished eating. He pulls me into his arms, and we lie down on the mattress curled up together. I grip his hand, willing him not to fall asleep even though I know he won't be able to fight the drugs.

I hear it when his breathing pattern finally shifts, and my breath hitches in panic.

A few minutes later, the door to the cell opens for the first time.

Our captor steps into the room. Given the monster he so obviously is, I expected him to be ugly, but he isn't. At least not on the outside. He's cruel beauty. A little shorter than Seven, probably six feet tall, and not quite as broad. In a fair fight, Seven would win no question, but I can see the clearly strong and lethal muscles under his T-shirt. He has strange light gray eyes that appear empty of everything and hair just a little lighter than Seven's. He's clean-shaven, where Seven has a growing beard, probably because of an inability to shave in here.

I grip Seven's hand harder as if he can protect me from our captor while unconscious.

The menacing stranger, the man who has insisted I, and I alone, call him master crosses the room to us. He hasn't demanded a title from Seven, and I'm starting to think his assessment is right. This man wants to make Seven a monster and me their whore.

He pries my fingers out of Seven's while I struggle against him and cry. "Please... please... don't hurt me." I've never been more afraid than I am now in this man's presence.

He tilts his head to the side like a curious puppy. Then he says, "Please, please don't hurt me, what?"

"M-Master," I say quickly.

He nods, satisfied with this answer but unwilling to offer me any reassurances to answer my plea.

He picks me up off the floor, then walks me to my corner on the other end of the room.

"Sit," he demands.

I slide wordlessly to the ground, the tears moving down my cheeks. Then he turns and crosses the floor to Seven. He grips the man by the shoulders, and drags him to the door.

"W-wait, where are you taking him?"

He looks up at me and smiles a hollow, soulless smile. "Oh, don't worry Pretty Toy, you'll get your turn soon enough."

He presses his thumb to a keypad, the door slides open, and he drags Seven out, leaving me alone in the cell.

4

It seems like hours go by while I'm in this classical elevator music hell alone. Finally, the door slides open, and he drags Seven back inside. I gasp at the sight of him, shirtless but still in jeans. Our captor tosses Seven on the mattress, lying on his stomach, revealing horrifying whip lashes across his back, several of them bleeding.

He's very still, and at first I'm terrified he's dead, but then I see his breath slowly moving in and out of him in a ragged labored way. I'm not sure if he passed out from pain or if he was drugged again. Then my captor's eyes move to me.

"Your turn, Pretty Toy."

I shake my head, the panic and tears back. "No, no please... Master, please... I'll do whatever you want... please... don't..." I look at the disaster that is Seven's back again.

My captor doesn't reply; he just walks slowly and calmly over to me.

"Please," I whimper. "I'm not as strong as him... I can't take... please..." I'm babbling. I can't think straight enough to make a clear sentence come out of my mouth. I'm just so scared. And I know none of what I say matters anyway. You can't reason with the devil.

I don't understand why. WHY? We did what he asked. And in this short time... he's already escalated his plans to torture. I'm sure I'll hyperventilate or faint when he reaches me.

"Stand up and come with me, Kate," he says.

I don't know why it should surprise me that he knows my name. I had my driver's license on me when he took me. If he undressed me and put me in this cell, of course he's gone through all my things.

I choke back another sob and use the wall to steady myself and stand. I know if I resist him, whatever he has planned can only be worse. I grip the bath towel around me, but he tugs it out of my grasp and off me until I'm standing inches from him, naked.

He grips my upper arm and leads me out of the cell. When we get out into the main house, I realize the finality of my fate. Even phrases like *ridiculous grandiose wealth* do not fully capture this situation. There's a level of resources where you know there's basically no limit to a person's power.

This guy has those kinds of resources. That kind of power. No one will ever find us. No one will ever free us. We're at the mercy of this monster for as long as he lets us live. And I'm not sure if a short time or a long time is better or worse under the circumstances.

The door to our cell is hidden behind a giant painting. The hallway alone in this place is breathtaking. High vaulted ceilings. Chandeliers that each probably cost about the same as a normal-sized house in the suburbs. We pass by windows, and outside the windows I see endless rolling hills. It's as though I've been transported to a whole other planet that only the three of us inhabit. Maybe it's a private island. I don't see any palm trees, but I really just have no idea at this point.

He has to have staff. A cleaning service. Something. There's no way he manages this on his own. So have there been others here while we've been here then? There must have been. If he isn't worried about us screaming and getting found out, the cell must be soundproof.

I could ask myself why someone with this much money would even do something like this. But why not? If you obviously have no conscience, after you get bored with all conventional accumulation of power, surely something like this is next.

At the end of this hallway, there's another door with a security panel. It's not hidden like our cell. I wonder if people ask what's behind this door. I'm sure others are curious, but I don't want to know. I don't want to go in there.

I struggle to get away from him, but his impossible grip only gets tighter. "Careful, now. Probably best not to irritate the psycho," he says.

At least he knows he's crazy. I'm not sure if that helps or only makes it worse.

Behind this new high-security steel door is a set of stairs that spiral down. The walls are white, and the stairs look like stairs in an office building. There are guide lights in the floor which offer the only illumination. The stairs seem to go down forever, and the further we go into this pit, the more claustrophobic I become.

It's some kind of sex dungeon. There are whips and paddles and floggers and canes. Clamps of various types and sizes. A box full of sex toys and blindfolds. Bondage equipment is scattered around the room. There's a large cage on one end of this endless underground space. And there's a bed, built with the explicit understanding that someone should be bound to it.

A part of me wishes I didn't know what all of this stuff was for. But I know. I'm crying again. It started before I even realized—traitorous tears making escape attempts down my cheeks.

I flinch when he wipes away a stray tear with his thumb. "Don't cry yet, Pretty Toy. I haven't even gotten started. Save your tears for the good part."

This only makes me cry harder, and the sinister smirk that inches up his cheek only confirms this was the reaction he was hoping for.

"You're here because you disobeyed me. You *both* disobeyed me."

Is he talking about the fact that we didn't immediately rush to fuck for his viewing pleasure when he first told us this was the price for food? Before I can ask this question, he continues.

"I told you, no names, Kate. But the first opportunity you got, the two of you huddled in your private shower and started whispering secrets. I may not have cameras in the bathroom, but I do have listening devices, one embedded in the shower in fact. Seven thought he could outsmart me. You have to be punished, Pretty Toy. I can't have this defiance."

"Master, please." I want to say it was Seven's idea, but my captor knows that already, and I can't stand the idea of betraying Seven, so I don't say anything more.

I jerk away when he strokes my hair.

"Don't worry. He took a greater punishment to protect you, and I always keep my word. You can handle what I'm about to do. I won't break your skin. I don't want to break my Pretty Toy after all, now do I?"

A long slow breath pushes its way out of me as my hysteria calms the tiniest fraction. I know he could be lying. I know he's evil. I know he's going to kill us when he's finished with his game, but I hold out hope that Seven really did take a harder punishment to give me a lighter one.

"Go lie down on the bed. On your stomach, arms and legs spread out like an X."

I can't do this. My body refuses to move to obey his command. There isn't enough air in this room. I can't. I know I have no choices here. He could get tired of me and kill me. The more easily I do whatever he wants the longer I'm sure I'll live, but I can't.

My body refuses to hold me up, and suddenly I'm on the ground, kneeling in front of him.

"Master please... please, I'm sorry I disobeyed. Please... don't hurt me. I promise I'll never do it again," I whimper. I am so pathetic right now. And a part of me knows this will only excite him, only drive him on, but I can't stop myself from begging and hoping for mercy he obviously doesn't possess.

He's cold and empty and completely unreachable, which only makes me feel more helpless. It makes me sick to think of Seven being beaten down here, knowing I would be next and that he can't truly protect me. No one can protect me.

"Kate," he says quietly. "I will only tell you once more. Get up and do what I said. Otherwise, I won't go easier on you, and Seven's suffering will have been for nothing. Is that what you want?"

"No, Master."

"Then obey me."

There's suddenly a hand next to my face, offering to help me stand. I take his hand and struggle to my feet. Then, having no other options, I go to the bed and lie down spread-eagled like he demanded.

I continue to cry hopelessly as he binds me to the bed with the attached restraints. They aren't for show or light play. A grown man couldn't get out of them on his own. I wonder if Seven was in this same spot only a little while ago or if our captor tied him to something else, maybe the giant X-shaped contraption leaning against one of the exposed brick walls.

I watch as he goes to the wall where the whipping implements hang, deciding what to use on me. He returns with a flogger. It's not the worst thing he could have picked, but he could still make it unbearable.

He sits on the bed beside me, and I flinch as he strokes my hair and then my back.

"Shhh, Pretty Toy."

He continues this soothing behavior until my body has no choice but to relax and calm under his touch. Something inside me gives up the fight to tense in his hands.

"That's a good girl," he soothes. His gaze holds mine as he says this.

His eyes really are beautiful. But they are so cold it's hard to look into them. They are gray like a storm. It's as though they were formed from pieces of ice. I'm certain there's nothing that could melt his gaze.

"As long as you're a good girl for me, I won't get a new toy to replace you."

He doesn't spell it out, but we both know what replacing me means. It doesn't mean he'll let me go.

I wish he wasn't so attractive. There's a twisted sick part of me that has a hard time completely understanding the danger he represents. This part of my mind can only process his beauty, and the way he's touching me isn't helping. These soothing gentle caresses are confusing.

My body arches into his touch as his hand strokes farther downward, until he's rubbing my ass. I should pull away even though there's nowhere for me to go. I want to pull away. I'm so scared right now, but I know he will do whatever he wants with me, and all my brain can process is that I'll be safe as long as I'm a good girl.

This thought repeats over and over in my mind like a mantra.

I don't really know this is true, but I cling to it anyway.

I'm caught off guard by the hard smack on my ass. It's followed by several more sharp blows in quick succession. I cry out, part from pain, part from shock at the sudden shift. But before I can tense up again, he's back to the soothing stroking.

Heat rises into my face as I realize my body has decided this is sexually exciting. Wetness floods between my legs. It's such a betrayal, this thing my body is doing to me. It was different with Seven. It's okay with Seven.

But this nameless man who took me off the street and locked me in a cell... I can't feel this when he touches me. I can't allow it. But my body doesn't care. My body equally craves the touch of both men. There is no either/or, it is only both/and. My eyes have greedily drunk both men's beauty and found them equally satisfying.

He spanks me again, this time the other cheek, and before he even gets to the gentle caress, even in the midst of the pain as I cry out, a deep throbbing ache begins between my legs. He rubs the sting out where he spanked me.

"Are you wet for me?" he asks.

I don't bother to lie because as bad as it is for me, I know the truth will please him. And that may be good for me.

"Yes, Master."

His hand moves between my legs, stroking my wet folds. I try not to grind against his hand. I try to just lie there, but when he presses a finger inside me, I begin to move against him. My body wants to fuck.

He chuckles. "Such a greedy toy. I like you."

I feel a perverse relief at this statement. If he were ugly, it would be easy to resist. My body would agree with my mind. If he were seriously hurting me, it would also be easy. But the pain he gives me is erotic, and his restraint only makes me want more.

There's something very wrong with me. I try to reason with myself that he didn't feed us for three days. I have so much adrenaline coursing through my body. I've been put in this completely helpless position, and instead of doing whatever grisly things psychos are supposed to do, he's giving me pleasure. It's incredibly hard to fight that, to be good.

Anyway, my definition of good and his definition are completely opposite. And the only definition that matters for my survival is his.

"Such a good girl. You are so responsive," he says as he continues to pet me between my legs.

I whimper, but otherwise, I can say nothing. I can do nothing but grind helplessly against his hand as he keeps my gaze trapped in his.

"Because you are such a good girl, I'm going to give you a choice. I can punish you with the flogger, or I can let you come. Tell me which do you want? Would you rather be whipped or come on my fingers?"

I squeeze my eyes shut even as I continue to move with his fingers. He pulls his hand away, and it takes everything inside me not to beg for more. Seven will touch me. I can get this from Seven. I won't have to feel like something is completely broken inside me because he's a good man. But I cannot give myself to *this* man except for survival. Not for pleasure. Not for sheer wanton desire. If there's a choice, I have to make the choice that won't make me feel so good.

"Open your eyes and look at me," he demands.

I open my eyes.

"Good. Now, choose, Kate. Pain or pleasure."

But I can't choose. It's demented to ask for pain, and even more wrong to ask for pleasure from this man. Or is it the opposite?

"Master, please... I can't."

"It's a hard choice, I get it," he says. He stands next to the bed, and a moment later, the flogger falls so hard against my back I lose my breath.

"That's pain," he says, as if this were a confusing sensation I wouldn't figure out on my own.

He climbs back onto the bed, straddling me, trailing kisses down my back, running his tongue over the welts his hand left only minutes ago. Then his fingers are inside me again, rubbing in the most intensely pleasurable way.

"This is pleasure," he says. "Do you want the demonstration again, or can you choose now?"

I know which he wants me to choose. If I deny him this and choose pain, he will make me regret it. Maybe he won't draw blood with the flogger, but it will hurt. What he just gave me was only a taste.

And so I fall. I submit. I give him what will please him even as it will break away a piece of my soul.

"Pleasure, Master."

"You're such a sweet whore," he says. His fingers fuck me harder as I buck shamelessly against his hand. It feels good, but I know I can't really come this way. I've never had that kind of orgasm—the one that comes from the inside. Part of me thinks they are a myth. Even so, I'm determined to fake it if necessary to please this dangerous man and save myself whatever pain I can.

But I don't have to. His other hand slips underneath me

and rubs my clit. He drives me harder and harder, my body growing wetter and more aroused with each pleasurable sensation he offers me.

"Come, Kate," he demands.

I wish he would call me Pretty Toy or even sweet whore. Not Kate. I can't stand to hear my name on his lips as I come apart in his hands.

The pleasure shatters me, and he is pleased.

"Good girl."

I shut my eyes as the shame crawls over me. I didn't just *let* this monster touch me, I wanted him to. My body craved him. If he had wanted to fuck me, I would have spread my legs wider and thrust my hips up at him in obedient invitation. I wouldn't have screamed or cried or begged him to stop.

This can't be me. This can't be who I am.

I think he'll untie me now and take me back to the cell, but he doesn't. Instead he goes to the box in the corner and comes back with a blindfold. I let him tie the dark cloth around my eyes without complaint because there's relief here. I don't have to look at him or be ensnared by that cold gray gaze. I can hide here.

"I'm not quite done with you. I want to test something."

He releases me from my bonds, then urges me onto my back and restrains me again, spread-eagled. I'm even more grateful for the blindfold now. This is too exposed. I want to beg him, but I'm not sure what I would be begging for. So I remain quiet and hide in this darkness he's offered me.

I hear his footsteps retreat. I hear things being moved around in that box he got the blindfold out of. Then he returns to me and sits beside me on the bed.

"I'm going to ask you some questions, Pretty Toy. And it's very important for your own safety that you tell me the truth. I'm good at spotting liars. You do not want to test me. Do you understand?"

"Y-yes, Master."

"Good. Do you masturbate?"

"Yes, Master," I whisper.

He releases one of my hands. "Show me how you do it."

"Please..." Even after all he's seen... even after how he's touched me and watched me come, I can't touch myself while he watches. I just... can't.

"I can still punish you," he says.

I don't want him to punish me. I'm too afraid after what I saw of Seven's back that if he gets started, if he gets too much of a taste for hurting me, he won't stop, and I won't survive it. Or if I do, I'll wish I hadn't.

My hand drifts down between my legs, and I begin to stroke my clit. I can feel his intense gaze on me. I feel like he's studying me, evaluating me—as though I'm getting some sort of performance review.

"Stop," he says.

My hand stills over my pussy.

"Do you not go inside?"

I shake my head.

"Why not?"

I've never had a discussion with anyone about this before. It's far too private, and I don't want this to be the person I tell this to. I know there's no right or wrong way to touch myself, but he makes me feel like there is, as though there's something childish in my technique.

"I only have an orgasm from the outside, so I don't see the point..."

He laughs out loud at this, and heat rises into my cheeks.

"What about vibrators? Do you use vibrators?" he asks.

"S-sometimes."

"On the inside or outside?"

"Outside."

"Hmmmm," he says. "I don't like that. We're changing that right now. I'm going to train you to come with penetration."

"And if I can't?" I ask, the fear threading my voice, making it come out small and quiet. Will he get a new toy, one he doesn't deem defective?

"You will. You've just never been taught properly."

If I weren't so afraid, I would be offended that this stranger thinks he understands my body and what it is and isn't capable of better than I do. I've tried masturbating that way before. It doesn't work. It makes me feel foolish as though I'm seeking an impossible thing that everybody else is faking, and I'm just too dumb to know it's all an act.

I jump when his hand encircles my wrist. He pulls my arm back over my head and secures me the way he had me.

"What if I can't?" I ask again. I know I shouldn't keep pushing this button, but I have to know. "A-are you going to kill me?"

Amusement laces his voice. "No, Kate, I'm not going to kill you. Killing is so unimaginative. I can't understand the soulless being who can't think of more interesting things to do than take life. I have far better things to do with you than kill you."

"Until you get tired of me," I say, wishing I could just shut up. I actually flinch when I say this because I'm afraid I'm pushing too far. I brace myself for the punishment I worry might still be coming.

But he just strokes my inner thigh. "Do you think I'm stupid, Pretty Toy?"

"N-no, Master."

"Only the stupid get bored. I'll never run out of ways to twist you to my will."

Somehow this possibility is more terrifying to me than death. Death promises an end. But my captor is offering the possibility that there will never be an end. And now I'm afraid there won't be. I was so busy worrying about him killing me that I didn't bother to worry about what would happen if he didn't.

He strokes my hair. "No more questions. Just feel. I'm going to teach your cunt how to obey me now."

I hear a buzzing, and I know he's turned the vibrator up to the highest setting. I want to tell him it will be too intense. I want him to start at the low setting, which I can handle.

As though he can read my mind, he leans in close to my ear and whispers, "I like sluts who can take intense hard vibrations. You will take it, and you will open your legs wider to take more. Do you understand?"

"Yes, Master."

Tears begin to slip out from beneath the fabric. Every time he speaks to me like this, my body wants him more. I can't cope with how he so easily turns me into his pliant plaything. I thought I would fight more.

I wanted to be someone who would fight. But I can't

fight this man. Some part of me knows it's because of the days of head games I've already experienced. The very real threat of starvation I experienced in the cell. I don't want that to happen ever again. And I don't want him to do to me what he did to Seven.

Is it so wrong that I want pleasure over pain even if it comes from a monster?

He spreads me open and presses the toy directly against my clit. I jerk away at the intensity, but he holds it there. I take slow, measured breaths.

He starts to move it up and down over my clit, and then he's dragging the pulsating tip down to my opening, then slowly back up again. He moves the toy over my entire pussy, from my most sensitive flesh, to my least sensitive. When I'm close to coming, he moves away from my clit and focuses on another area with far fewer nerve endings.

This torment goes on forever, and after a while, I'm arching and grinding, moving with the toy. He slips it briefly inside me, then out again. Then he's teasing me everywhere but my clit. He's gotten me so close to the edge, but he refuses to give me sensation where I need it to get off.

"Beg me to come," he says.

I don't bother to fight. There's no point. We both know I want this, but I thought he was going to fuck me with it.

"Please, Master, let me come." It's the second time I've said these words today, and to two different men. It makes me feel like such a whore.

He begins to work the vibrator inside me, even as I desperately want it on my clit. I'm so wet and throbbing and needy right now. I've never been this aroused before.

I've never been tormented this long and kept on the edge of pleasure like this.

He fucks me with it, dragging it in and out so slowly I want to scream: *I can't come this way!* Then he's on the outside again, teasing my opening, running the toy over my labia, barely grazing my clit.

I'm crying now. "Please..."

"The only way you're coming is if the vibrator is inside you. I don't care if it takes hours to get there. You will get there. It's the only way it's happening, so your body better figure it out."

It's moving inside me again, slow, then fast, then slow again. This tease goes on forever. I'm trembling with my need. I want to beg him *please please just touch my clit. Please I'll do anything.* But I can't say those shameful words.

I wonder how long he'll do this before he gives up and punishes me for not being able to do what he wants me to do.

But then suddenly with no warning, I arch off the bed, my body bucking wildly against the vibrator as he fucks me harder with it. The pleasure builds from somewhere deep inside me and explodes in the most shattering orgasm I've ever had.

He turns the toy off. I lie there for a moment, shaking, unable to believe what just happened, unable to comprehend that the one thing I've wanted so desperately to experience I only somehow managed in captivity.

A moment later the tip presses at my lips.

"Clean it," he orders.

My tongue darts out and licks my own juices off the toy.

"Good girl. I told you, you just needed to be taught how to come that way. You just needed patience. It will get easier each time. And then it will be my cock taking you there."

He lies down next to me and strokes my face and the side of my neck for what feels like forever, and I hate myself just a little bit for wanting him to never stop.

5

When I'm returned to the cell, it's silent. No music. Seven is still unconscious. I was gone probably less than an hour, but I'm still worried because he hasn't woken yet. The cell door opens again, and I flinch, but our captor only leaves clean clothes for Seven. None for me, of course. I'm never getting clothes again, and he made it very clear to me before bringing me back that he doesn't want to see the towel on me anymore.

I go to the bathroom and take the first aid kit out of the cabinet. When I return, I put everything on the ground next to the mattress and sit down. I gently touch a part of his shoulder that isn't damaged and shake him.

"Master," I say. Our captor was very clear about how I am to address my co-captive. It doesn't matter what Seven and I think about it, it isn't worth it to disobey. And after the darkly twisted pleasure I just received in the dungeon, the smallest part of me wants to follow these orders even beyond the terror of what might happen if I don't.

He groans and shifts.

I stroke the side of his face. "Just be still. I'm going to bandage you up."

Seven becomes alert, his eyes flying open. "Did he hurt you?"

"N-no. Not like you. I'm okay." I'm not *really* okay, but I'm not bleeding.

"Don't call me that," he says. So he heard the first word I spoke to him.

"I have to. It's what he wants. Don't shame me for..."

He reaches out, his hand gripping mine, stopping me.

"I would never shame you, but I can't stand to see you demeaned like this."

"I know."

I gently extricate my hand from his and start cleaning the marks on his back. I have a complicated swirl of emotions surrounding Seven. In such a short period of time, I'm starting to feel things for him that I don't think I should, things I'm not sure are real. It's the trauma bonding of an extreme situation.

Not that I wouldn't be attracted if we'd met in a normal way. I would be. And I'm sure in time, I would come to know and understand his very appealing protective nature. But it feels like letting myself feel things for Seven is all a part of a complex game that I don't yet fully understand the rules for. And I'm afraid if I let myself care for him, it only gives me more to lose.

He winces but doesn't cry out as I apply an antibiotic cream to his back. I feel so guilty that I don't have any marks. I know it would upset Seven if my skin had been broken, but it feels wrong that he got all this pain and damage, and I got earth shattering pleasure.

The original shame I felt at this is completely overwhelmed by the shame I feel now at the very different experience I got in the dungeon. I unroll the gauze across the marks that are open, and tape it down with medical tape. Some of his whip lashes are just red, not bloody, so I leave those alone except for the cream.

Seven struggles to sit up. He lets out a pained hiss as he leans against the wall.

"Maybe you shouldn't do that," I say.

He shakes his head. "No. It's cool to the touch. It's better now. I'm fine." His hazel gaze cuts to mine, concerned. "What did he do to you?"

I look away. "Just leave it."

The voice of our captor comes out over the speaker again. "I gave our girl her first vaginal orgasm. It's too bad you missed the show, the way she bucked against the vibrator... the way she *begged* me. It was beautiful."

My face flames at this, and I can't look at Seven.

"You sick fuck!" Seven says.

For the smallest moment, I worry those words are directed at me, but when I look back at him, I see his face is turned up toward the camera.

"You were the one who wanted her to have a lighter punishment. You made a trade. Do you regret the choice now that you know what *lighter punishment* means?" our captor mocks.

Seven's voice comes out so cold it frightens me. "You will make a mistake. And when you do, I will kill you."

The only response from our captor is laughter. "I really

love this noble act you've got going."

"It's not an act."

"Of course it is. Everything is an act. Everything is a game," our captor says. "Ready for lunch, pets? You've been so good I didn't even drug it this time."

Bottles of water are dropped through the slot. Since Seven is hurt, I go over to the food slot and take the plates as they come through. Both plates are white this time. It's ham and cheese sandwiches, pickles, and potato chips. Is it really lunchtime?

I know it's at least day because of my time outside the cell, the windows we passed.

We eat experimentally as if we don't trust our captor's assurances about the state of the food, but there really are no drugs this time. So he must not be coming in. In fact, several days pass without him coming in or even speaking to us except to announce food so one of us can go get it as it's passed through the slot.

We're fed three times a day, and the food matches the time of day. Typical breakfast, lunch, and dinner fare seem to be served at the appropriate times.

I find myself weirdly grateful to our captor for this way to mark time. Each night, Seven and I sleep curled up together on the mattress. We turn the bathroom light out to sleep and lie together in total darkness.

In this darkness and privacy, Seven touches me. We never had a conversation about it. He didn't ask. I didn't say no. And he hasn't asked for the favor to be returned. I feel somehow shy about touching him back. So I just lie there under the cover of darkness as he caresses me and kisses my throat.

He starts out innocent each time. Safe places. My hair and face. My arms and legs. But he always finds his way to my breasts and then between my thighs, which I spread open for him every night without fail. He strokes me until I come, trying to keep my desperate panting and moans quiet but always failing. Then he whispers in my ear "Sleep."

And I do.

My dreams are intense and erotic. Usually it's Seven I dream about. But sometimes it's our captor. I try not to think about those dreams. Seven is okay. Our captor isn't. Even so, the dreams with cold light gray eyes are more intense because they are more wrong.

What I do for Seven each day isn't sexual. I take care of his back. I help him bathe without getting the bandages wet, and then I change them, applying more ointment to the whiplashes that still need them.

Each morning there are new clothes for Seven and the old clothes have been taken out. There seems to be a rotation of three pairs of jeans and T-shirts for him since he doesn't sleep naked. He never wears the T-shirt anymore. I think he only wears the jeans because he doesn't want me to feel threatened by his near-constant erection around me.

I've slept through this strange clothing exchange every night but one. One night I heard the door slide open. I held my breath. No light ever came on, which makes me wonder if our captor is using night vision goggles. He never touched me. I just heard a few soft sounds, and then he was gone.

6

I t's the fifth day of this routine. We just had our breakfast. Seven is in the bathroom running a bath in the large jacuzzi tub. When he steps out into the cell, the bandages are gone. There will be scars, but he's healed and no longer in any pain. And thankfully, they didn't get infected.

"Come take a bath," he says. I think I hear an unspoken *with me* in there.

I've grown to not only trust Seven but to feel comfortable with him. I no longer try to hide my body from his hungry gaze. I'm not sure why our captor hasn't escalated things, why he hasn't touched me again, or why he hasn't made Seven fuck me for his amusement again. And while I'm grateful, there are the dreams that say there's an animal part of me that wants more to happen—that is ready for more to happen, even though the civilized part of me rebels.

It's only in the absence of the sexual demands of our

captor that I learn to crave it. To want it. Maybe it's partly because of the way Seven has unknowingly stoked this fire within me each night as he touches me, and I open and surrender to his questing hands. I don't know why Seven does it. I think it's some sort of strange comfort.

Or maybe he wants me too much. Maybe fucking me that first time has stoked a fire in him that now won't go out, either. Maybe he reasons that giving me pleasure is less evil than taking it from me. After all, what does he get out of this arrangement?

I get up and follow Seven into the bathroom. He strips off his jeans and gets into the tub. He crooks a finger at me and points to the water. The way he looks at me now is entirely carnal. He doesn't want to just take a bath. And neither do I.

I climb into the tub with him, leaning back against his chest. His erection presses against my lower back.

"Seven?"

His hand clamps over my mouth.

"Shhh. Listening devices, remember?"

I nod, and he pulls his hand away.

"Master?" I think if I quickly correct my error, our captor might not punish me for the mistake.

I feel Seven's cock go harder beneath me. He may be upset by my degradation on a purely moral level. But he likes it when I use that word. He likes that word directed at him. It turns him on. It doesn't mean he wants it exactly—especially if he thinks I don't want it—but it *does* excite him, which makes me feel just a little bit better about it. Because it excites me, too.

"Why do you think he's doing this?" I ask. We both

know I don't mean why is he holding us captive. *He's a psycho* doesn't really need further explanation. No, the question is why is he just feeding us and leaving us alone, not taunting us, not messing with us. Is he bored? I remember he said smart people don't get bored, and I know he thinks of himself as smart.

"I'm not sure. But I don't like it. I don't think we can trust this peace and safety."

I tense in Seven's arms, but I think the same.

We don't say anything more. There's been a silence between us for most of our time together in the cell, but it's a comfortable silence. It's a silence that feels much safer than talking.

He takes a raspberry shower gel and squeezes some into his hands and starts to wash me. I sigh in contented pleasure leaning into his touch as he massages the gel into my skin. I shouldn't feel this good being held captive. Seven is slow and thorough. His hands linger longer over my breasts, my ass, and between my legs. His fingers slip inside me, and I buck against him.

"Wait..." I say, "what about you?"

I wanted to return the favor and wash him, though maybe not with raspberry. I think I saw some peppermint in the cabinet. Even though I find myself too shy to initiate anything, to touch him without him guiding me to, I really want to touch him. I remember that first day in the shower. I want to lick that 'V' again.

"I showered while you were still sleeping. We don't need to bathe me. Turn around and straddle me."

We've gone days with him only giving, never taking. His restraint has been admirable. Each day he hasn't asked anything of me, I've grown to trust him a little more. But we both have needs, and we're here together. It seems foolish not to take our pleasures where we can get them. Especially if we'll probably die here.

I know our captor says he won't get bored and that killing is unimaginative, but what does he plan to do with us when he's finished? Because someday he will be finished.

I start to turn around to do what Seven has asked, but his hand on my hip stills me.

"Wait, are you on birth control?"

He could have asked the question when we fucked a few days ago, but we were hungry and not exactly in the right frame of mind for that thought process. And it didn't matter anyway, if we wanted to eat. He knows I can't be on the pill. Is he hoping I had the shot?

"No, but I don't need it. I can't have children."

"How do you know?"

"Trust me. I know. I had to see a lot of doctors when I was a teenager. They discovered an abnormality in my uterus. It wasn't directly related to the problem I was having but they stumbled on it. I've been this way since birth. The short version is I can't have kids."

"There's no treatment or surgery?"

"There really isn't anything they can do in my case. Some women with milder abnormalities have lots of miscarriages but have at least a small chance of maintaining a pregnancy, but mine is too malformed. It just can't happen. I'm not built right."

At first I don't realize I've started crying. Seven strokes my back.

"Shhh. I'm sorry. I didn't mean to upset you. I just didn't want to take more risks than we had to."

"It's okay."

Is this why he hasn't taken? Even though we're being fed on a regular schedule, I'm still bait. I'm still naked, locked in an enclosed space with a man strong enough to take what he wants. And he would never get caught by any outside authorities because we both know we will never be free.

If he wasn't afraid I'd get pregnant—with whatever added horror *that* might entail—would he still have had this saintly self-control?

He's stroking my hair. "Do you want me?" he asks.

He never asked if I wanted him to stroke me to orgasm each night in the dark. My legs falling open when he reached my thighs was enough for him. But this is obviously different.

"Yes, Master."

A sharp intake of breath is his only reply. He *does* like it when I call him that. He doesn't want to like it, but he likes it.

"You know you don't have to call me that when we're alone."

"I have to call you something, and he won't allow names. It doesn't bother me."

"Climb on top of me and ride me," he says, choosing not to address the fact that calling him master *doesn't bother me.*

It's such a weird thing for me to have said, but it *doesn't* bother me. In the time we've been captive together I've started to feel this strange submissive urge toward him. I like the idea of him having this power. It makes me feel safer even though I know I'm not.

I turn and straddle him, sliding down over his huge cock. I don't know how many times we'll do this, but I'm sure I'll never get used to his size.

"You are so fucking tight. How are you so fucking tight?"

I shrug. "No children?"

"Good point."

I close my eyes and slowly start to move. I brace my hands against his chest. His hands come up and close over mine.

"Open your eyes. Look at me," he says.

I open my eyes and hold his hazel gaze. This can't really be called fucking. It's making love. I'm not sure how I feel about that, but it's what it is. It's slow and sweet, but the angles are all wrong. It's too hard to do this in this tub. Seven realizes the same thing.

"Let's move to the shower," he says.

"Okay." I get up on shaking legs, and he helps me out of the tub. He pulls the plug and lets that water drain as he moves us into the huge shower. He doesn't turn the water on. He just pulls me into the enclosed glass space with him. Without a word, he bends me forward until my hands are resting flat on the ground.

I gasp when he enters me from behind. I've never done this in this position. The penetration is so deep that I feel this excited flip in my stomach with every thrust. I've secretly wanted his cock inside me again for so long that I don't need him to tease me or work me up. I'm already wet and ready for him.

The wait, the tightness, the angle, it's all too much for him, too. He drives into me with such ferocity it steals my breath. No sweet words of endearment are exchanged between us. We are no longer making love. We are fucking. Or he is fucking me. There is something animal and wild in this moment. His ability to resist this has frayed at the edges. *He* has frayed at the edges.

He lets out a harsh guttural sound when he comes, then he pulls out of me. I think I might cry. I know he didn't mean it this way, but I feel like he just used me for his own pleasure without anything for me—like he just masturbated inside my body. A part of me is turned on, but another part is pissed being left like this, so desperate and needing.

I know I'm technically way ahead on the orgasm count, but still.

He steps out of the shower, and I just stand there for several minutes, numb. How is it that what happened in the dungeon with that sick psychopath feels like less of a violation somehow than this? I just had a bath, but I feel like I need another one.

I'm about to turn on the water and bathe again when he says, "Come out here."

I step out of the shower to find he's laid several large thick bath towels down on the tile floor. He motions for me and I join him.

"Lie down."

I wonder if these short sharp orders are a result of hearing the word *Master* on my lips. It's as though this word flips a switch inside him, and suddenly he wants to possess me.

I lie down on my back. He settles between my legs and languidly caresses and licks me until I come, my legs shaking from the force of my pleasure. I now feel so stupid for doubting him, for thinking he would leave me unfulfilled and just use me. I let out a long contented sigh as he strokes my belly.

He gets up and comes back a few minutes later with a warm wet wash cloth which he uses to clean me from our mingling fluids slipping down my thighs. I am falling for this man, and I no longer care if it's real.

I FEEL STRANGELY SELF-CONSCIOUS WHEN WE GO BACK INTO the cell. Seven has jeans on again. He sits on his side of the cell beside the mattress, and I sit on mine. This draws an odd look from him.

"Don't you want to come lie down with me?" he asks. He looks almost hurt by this, as though I'm rejecting him.

I don't know why I went to my old spot. Before I can answer, sounds are coming out of the speaker. It's the sounds of him fucking me in the shower—that wild animal sound he made when he came. There's silence for a moment, and then it's my recorded moans of pleasure filling the cell.

Then the voice speaks for the first time outside of meals in five days. "It's about time," he says. "I thought you two would never fuck on your own. It was like watching pandas in captivity."

I swallow hard, my gaze going to Seven's.

"Congratulations, pets," our captor says. "You've

unlocked the next level. I know he's been touching you at night. The cameras have a night vision setting, but you can't level up unless you fuck on your own. I'm so excited."

I don't know why my subconscious mind has been romanticizing and sending me erotic dream imagery of our captor, but suddenly all the fear of him is back in a single moment.

There's a light tinkling metallic sound on the floor under the food slot, and I see that a key has been dropped onto the ground.

"Pretty Toy," our captor says, "chain him up."

I look at Seven, my eyes wide. Somehow I'd thought he would have to feed us and give Seven the drugs before he could come in here. Somehow I'd been living in the false security that I was safe at all other times inside this cell. He can't come in here otherwise without being overpowered unless he brings a weapon, and I know Seven would rush him, even if he pointed a gun.

This option hadn't occurred to me.

There's a loud sigh over the speaker as I remain frozen, staring at that key.

"No more food comes through the slot until you chain him up. You already know I can wait you out, so I suggest the two of you cooperate. There's no point starving yourself and suffering more. Don't you agree?"

The look in Seven's eyes is stark, not because he's about to allow himself to be chained up, but because it leaves me vulnerable and because it was his need to fuck me without orders to do so that *unlocked the next level.*

I struggle to stand and cross the floor to the food slot. I stare at the shiny silver key for several minutes as though trying to teleport it out of this house so we'll be safe. But the key stubbornly refuses to disappear under the urgency of my thoughts.

Finally, I pick it up and cross the room to Seven.

"I'm sorry," he whispers.

"You couldn't have known."

"I should have."

My hands are shaking too hard to unlock the shackles on the wall, so Seven takes the key from me and unlocks them. He gives it back before locking the first shackle on himself. He holds out his other wrist. I'm crying now.

I shake my head. "I can't." I turn up toward the camera. "Are you going to hurt him?"

"Of course not," the voice says. "He didn't break any rules."

"A-are you going to hurt me?"

"Address me properly," he says. I know he heard everything in the bathroom. Of course he must be angry that I would so easily and without prompting call Seven *Master*, but refuse the title to him. It wasn't intentional. I would never intentionally piss this guy off. I'm just too scared to think.

"I'm sorry, Master."

But he doesn't answer my question. He only says, "Obey, Pretty Toy."

I look to Seven as if he can offer me some guidance. There are no choices here. If I don't chain him up, we'll just go for days without food until I finally give in, and then I'll be half starved on top of whatever is about to happen here. But if I do lock the other chain around Seven's wrist... that door is going to open.

I can't cope with the idea of that door opening and that swirling mass of darkness coming into this cell with us.

I pace back and forth, my hands shaking so violently I drop the key.

"You're only making this harder on yourself," our captor says. His voice is so calm and reasonable I want to scream.

"Look at me," Seven says, careful not to use my name, careful not to break the rules.

I look into his eyes. I'm struggling to calm my crying, struggling to breathe.

"It's okay," Seven says.

It's not okay, and we both know it. But I have no real choice. I take a deep shuddering breath and lock the second shackle around his wrist. That click is the loudest sound I've ever heard.

The chains are long enough that he's still able to pull me into his arms. He holds me, cradling my head against his chest like he did that first day in the shower. His other hand strokes my back.

"Shhhh," he soothes. But I can't stop crying.

I flinch when I hear the metal door slide open and the sound of our captor walking into the room. I squeeze my eyes shut and press harder against Seven's chest.

"Come to me, Pretty Toy."

I hold on to Seven harder. I can't go to that monster.

"Don't hurt her," Seven warns.

"Or what? You'll do something heroic? Kate, what did I say about names in here? I distinctly heard you say his name in the bathroom. If you're smart, you will step out of his arms and beg me for mercy."

Seven's grip on me tightens like he's just made up his mind to never let me go, to never let our captor have me. I wish it were that simple, but I know it's not.

Our captor comes closer, standing on the side my face is turned toward.

"Open your eyes, sweet whore."

I bite back my sobs and open my eyes to see that cold gray gaze sliding into me. Something dark inside me awakens, and I feel the throbbing start between my legs. I try to make it stop, but it won't, even as I'm so fucking scared of him.

My gaze drops to the cane in his hand.

"Master, please, please..."

But he's not concerned with me right now. He's turned his attention to Seven. He props the cane against the wall and pulls a syringe out of his pocket. He removes the protective cap from the needle and pushes the air out, tapping the side of the needle.

"You can release her to me, or I can inject you with a sedative and take her. She'll be punished worse if I have to do that."

I feel Seven's arms slacken around me in defeat.

"Good. Now, Kate, come, throw yourself on my mercy."

I know what he wants from me. There is this almost psychic link that formed between us that day in the dungeon. I've had to start trying to think like him to survive this total mind fuck he's got me under. I pull myself from the warm, safe circle of Seven's arms, turn away from him, and kneel in front of our captor. I think of him as our captor, but the thought that really keeps coming to the front of my mind is *my master*.

I've been trying so hard for days to not think that phrase, to not let it burrow inside my soul and set up camp there. But it's useless. This man owns me, and both Seven and I know it. He may also own Seven in a sense, but he has this twisted desire to bring my would-be protector over to his side of the good and evil divide, leaving me alone, helpless, and at the mercy of both of them.

I want to convince myself that this isn't possible, but look at how he's already conditioned me. And I know how much Seven wants me and how the word *Master* affects him. It's only a matter of time before my one safe haven is gone.

I let the tears fall because there's no point in being brave. I don't think bravery wins me points with this man. He wants to watch me break and crumble at his feet. And so I do. I give him what he wants. I let him see this absolute vulnerability and how broken I am. I think that if I do this, somehow I can hold onto a small piece of myself and hide it and keep it safe within me.

"Master, please. I beg you. Forgive me. I'm sorry I disobeyed. Please... spare me."

He chuckles. "Oh, yes, my sweet whore. You know exactly the way I like it."

He derives a real pleasure from these words I speak, these tears I cry, my total despair kneeling at his feet. He seems to get the kind of satisfaction from this that most men get from a blow job.

I flinch when he starts to stroke my hair.

He reaches down, takes my hands in his, and pulls me to stand. Then he spins me around so that my back is pressed against his front, so that I'm exposed, facing Seven. He holds my throat in a possessive grip with one hand as the other moves slowly over my body—as though he's displaying a pretty object he intends to sell for the right price.

"Look at her," he says to Seven. "She's so fucking perfect. Already she's so perfect. You will soon come to appreciate all the work I'm doing. Watch her." Then he whispers in my ear. "Look at him. Do you see the lust? He's not your hero. Remember that, Pretty Toy. Remember that when he goes dark. Because he will."

There's anger at our captor in Seven's eyes, but beneath that I do see it. I see the lust. I see the animal way he wants me. One side of him wants to break free of these chains and protect me—and he does make a valiant effort as he pulls on them with all the strength he has. But the shadow inside him wants to feed.

"Now, I need you to be a very good girl for me and go stand next to your chains facing the wall. It's time for your punishment."

"Please," I whimper. I'm falling apart in his arms. I can barely hold myself up as the terror of that cane grips me.

"Shhhh," he says, "I'm very pleased with your begging." He cups his hand against my mound, pulling me back against him. I feel his hard length pressing into my bare skin through his pants. "You've earned some mercy. Now go, before you lose it again."

He releases me, and I stumble a few steps forward. Seven reaches out and catches me. His thumb strokes over my arm—a barely perceptible gesture of comfort. I look away from his gaze, right myself, and go to the other end of the cell, turning to face the wall.

When our captor comes to me, he's collected the cane and the silver key. I think I may hyperventilate as he unlocks the shackles and locks my wrists into them. These are smaller than Seven's for much smaller wrists—like mine.

"Press your hands flat against the wall, up near your face to support yourself," he growls in my ear. "And do not move them. You're getting five."

I whimper as he slowly and gently drags the tip of the cane over my back. I find myself arching toward these soothing pleasurable sensations, but then he pulls away.

The pain from the first strike across my ass makes all of my nerve endings cringe, trying desperately to escape his reach. The instrument he just used to give me comfort has transformed back to its true form—a thing to be feared. My scream bounces off the walls of the cell. There's no way I can handle four more of these.

"M-master, please..."

"Ooops. I promised you some mercy. I forgot. It's so easy to forget rules. I'm sure you can relate." His voice drips with acid.

"I'm sorry! I swear I'll never speak his name again." It pains me to say this because I really like the sound of Seven's name on my lips. When I forget it's a number, the simple sound of it is comforting and sensual, like a far more sophisticated and worldly Kevin.

"Good girl," my master says.

The next four strikes are tolerable but still leave their searing impression into my flesh. Tears slide down my cheeks in response to each harsh kiss of the cane. My body trembles, but I can handle it. It doesn't feel like the world is on fire. It doesn't feel like *I* am on fire.

This time he keeps his word and stops after the fifth strike. He leans the cane against the wall and begins to carefully rub the welts he left. Then he's kneeling behind me, his tongue trailing over them, causing me to shudder against his warm questing mouth. He presses a kiss against my skin and rises.

"You will be a good girl from now on, won't you?"

"Yes, Master."

"Good." He presses his hand between my legs and chuckles. "I knew you would be wet for me after your punishment."

He strokes between my legs for a moment. I try not to grind against his hand, but I fail. He stops, only needing to make the point that my body belongs to him whether or not my mind has fully caught up yet.

He unlocks the shackles, and I slide bonelessly to the floor, leaning against his leg for support. But he's far from done with me. I feel the energy in him change, and I brace myself for whatever is coming next.

I chance a glance at Seven. He looks broken, like he was the one who just got caned.

"Let's play a different game," he says. "Today it's lady's choice. I can fuck you while Seven watches, or I can give him a punishment to spare you this indignity."

"I'll take the punishment," Seven says without hesitation even though he just truly healed from the last one.

"Are you a lady? I wasn't asking you. That's not how this game works. *She* gets to choose."

I bite my lip, willing myself not to cry anymore. I hate

how much I cry now, how weak and fragile I've become in so short a time. He steps away from me, and I manage to catch myself, my hands bracing against the floor.

I look up and his cold gray gaze settles on me. He knows what I'll choose. I can't let him beat Seven. I can't *choose* for him to beat Seven. He already took a punishment to spare me.

"I'll take the punishment," Seven says, more insistent, this time to me. "It's okay. I can't watch him force himself on you."

Our captor laughs at this. "Oh, believe me, it won't be forced. Our Kate has a secret. She wants me. And she hates herself for it. But she *does* want me. We have a connection. I felt it. I felt the way she surrendered in the dungeon and gave herself over to me."

"She's terrified of you!"

"Yes. But her desire runs far deeper than her fear. And she's so grateful for the way I awakened her to a new level of pleasure she didn't even know she could feel." He turns to me then. "Tell me, Kate, and be honest, you know how I hate lies. You've thought about what it would be like when I fucked you. You've gotten aroused by it. Haven't you?"

I can't stand to say these words out loud, but I'm sure he will punish me again much worse if I lie. "Y-yes, Master."

"So, see, Seven... it actually won't be some big horror for her to let me inside her pretty pussy. What bothers her is that you will watch and maybe judge her just a little for what a dirty whore she is. And you *will* watch. I would hate for her to have to degrade herself like this only for you to cheat on our game. Then I'll have to fuck her *and* punish you."

"Listen to me, you don't have to do this. I'll take the punishment," Seven says, his hazel gaze capturing mine before I look away again.

I notice he's not saying my name. He knows what will happen if he does.

Our captor notices it, too. "Oh yes," he says. "I forgot. You don't have anything to call her. Hmmm. If I'm going to share ownership, you need a pet name for her. How do you feel about Slut?"

Seven practically roars. He's so angry that for a moment I'm almost more afraid of him than our captor. Despite his evil, our captor remains calm, calculated. He doesn't do anything without thinking five moves ahead. But Seven is pure, raw emotion. Pure anger. He jerks on the chains so hard a part of me thinks he actually can pull them out of the wall and somehow save me... save us.

But the chains are solid, bolted into the concrete, too strong for even the greatest anger and protective instinct to break.

"Okay. No Slut," our captor says. "You could have just vetoed the choice. For fuck's sake. You are such a drama queen." He paces like he's really thinking this through. "So something cute then? Something sweet? How about Kitten?"

Seven catches my gaze, and there's a question there. I nod. I like Kitten. And I would especially like it coming out of Seven's mouth, which makes it seem impossible that our captor will actually allow us this small kindness.

"Excellent. Kitten it is, then. See how easy that was?

Not everything has to be a fight, Seven. Not every discussion is a dragon for you to slay. We can come to terms you and I. We can share her. We already know how much you enjoy her. So let's enjoy her together."

Seven ignores the taunt and turns back to me. "Kitten, let me take the punishment. You have a choice. Use it."

I shake my head. "I can't, Master."

He flinches almost imperceptibly when I say this, but I'm afraid if I don't use the title, more punishment will come to me.

"Good girl," our captor says softly, reaching down to pet my hair. "You're learning."

I lean into his touch without thought.

Every word out of his mouth is true. I don't emotionally want him, but my body craves him. A twisted part of me does want to know what it feels like to have him moving inside of me. How will he fuck me? Will he be rough like Seven was in the shower? Or will he maintain this calculated calm?

And I do hate myself for this. He is evil. He can do any terrible thing he wants to either of us. This man quite literally has no soul. No conscience. There's nothing behind his eyes beyond the simple amusement of his game and we, his pawns. We are the pieces he moves around his game board with impunity.

I can only hope he truly doesn't get bored and that his creativity doesn't turn to brutal torture. It feels like he's inside my head. I'm sure he studies and analyzes me with the help of his cameras. Always. He studies Seven, too.

He knows exactly which button to push with me and exactly when and how to push it. This is the most terrifying thing about him—how smart he is. I've never known somebody this smart. If he had been violent from the start with me, I might have quickly rushed to obey him, but it would have been only out of fear.

And I *do* fear him, more than anything I've ever feared. But he's right; the desire is louder. And it wouldn't be there if he hadn't been so patient, so gentle with me so far. Yes, he's punished me, and it hurt, but he hasn't done any of the extremely violent things he could have so easily done. And he didn't rape me. And it isn't because he isn't capable of these things. I saw that clearly enough on Seven's back.

All of this combines with his physical beauty to create this gratefulness and need—this sick part of me that finds myself *wanting* to please him to pay him back for these small kindnesses.

But I don't kid myself about this. He wants to break me. He *is* breaking me. But he wants to do it with pleasure. That's the cruelest way to do it. I know this, but still I want him. And though I feel a deep shame at the idea of Seven watching me fall... the throbbing wetness, this continuing and growing ache between my legs tells me, part of me wants him to watch.

"Make your choice, Kate. Let me fuck you while Seven watches, or let our noble hero take another punishment for you."

"Kitten..." Seven says. It comes out a low rumbling growl.

Our captor is right. There's this bizarre connection between us. I know what I'll choose, and I know exactly how he wants me to phrase it. I know what will please him the most to hear.

So I look up at him, still kneeling on the floor. My lip trembles as I say, "Please, Master, fuck me."

"Good girl," he says, a slow, amused smile spreading across his face.

I barter with myself in this moment. I promise myself I will only give my softer feelings to Seven. I will only *love* Seven, because I know I am beginning to love him. Who wouldn't? He's perfect in every way. I'm safe with him.

But I will never love our captor. I will give him my body. I will please him. I will do whatever he asks of me, but I won't let myself feel the things that are okay with Seven. I won't give him my mind or my soul.

"I can't think how I want to take you. Any requests, Seven?"

Seven is taking slow, measured breaths. I can't reassure him that I'm okay with our captor fucking me. It sounds insane even locked safely inside my own mind. And I'm not sure I want to see the look on Seven's face if he believed me.

He doesn't respond to our captor's taunts, and so I'm placed on my hands and knees, facing Seven. I hear a zipper, then pants falling to the floor. I assume he removes his T-shirt as well but I can't bring myself to turn around and look at him. If he's as perfect under that T-shirt as I suspect, I don't think I could cope with the level of lust I might feel if I paused to truly drink in his beauty.

He presses a strangely sweet kiss to the small of my back, causing me to forget for the smallest fraction of a second what he is... why we're here. A second later, his hand is moving between my legs, my arousal coating his fingers.

"She's so wet," he says. It's almost an accusation, as though it's yet another thing I should be punished for.

I'm breathing hard, almost panting. I can't believe how turned on I am. It's wrong to feel this way, but something about my time in this cell, the realization of the hopelessness of the situation, it gives me permission to feel what I feel, no matter what that feeling might be.

Three days of hunger. Five days of peace and solace. Quiet interspersed with classical music and evil sarcasm. I am the farthest thing in the world from free, but I am free of one thing... the moral judgment or pity of the outside world. Even Seven's possible judgment can't touch me in this moment because I'm so aroused by the idea of him watching me like this as our captor takes me on the floor of the cell.

His hand snakes around my throat, pulling me back. "Look at him," our captor says to me. "You will hold his gaze while I fuck you. Do you understand?"

"Y-yes, Master."

But Seven is looking away, his gaze trained on a distant spot on the wall.

"Seven..." he warns. "Look at her. If you look at her, I'll be gentle. If you don't..." He doesn't need to finish the last part of his threat.

Seven turns his face toward me, his intense hazel gaze locked on mine as our captor slides easily into me. He's big, like Seven, but my body has decided to welcome him eagerly, not even asking for time to adjust to his size.

I moan as he slams his cock into me. It's not exactly gentle, but it's also not exactly unpleasant. I watch Seven watching me as I'm fucked and used at the whim of the twisted stranger who holds our lives in his hands. His fingers dig into my hips as he thrusts.

"Even if you can, don't come this time," he growls. "This one is *only* for me."

There's a low, hard flip in my stomach, and I feel myself go wetter as he slides even more effortlessly in and out of me. What is wrong with me? When Seven left me wanting in the bathroom, I felt hurt. This man does it, and it feels like Christmas.

I know he'll let me come; he's just decided that this time I'm to give him everything and take nothing other than the satisfaction of his pleasure. And the part of me too broken to know it's broken excitedly complies with these demands.

He falls into a hypnotic rhythm, and I find myself opening to him more, so much so that I feel the teasing edges of a potential orgasm licking at my insides. I feel like I could chase it and catch it if I tried, but I let it flutter away like a wayward butterfly as he lets out a harsh groan, taking his pleasure and spilling into me.

"Look at him, Pretty Toy."

My eyes haven't left Seven's, but that's not what I'm being asked to look at.

"Look how hard he is. Maybe he's not such a hero after all. Crawl to him. I want to watch you suck his dick."

Our captor slides out of me and puts his jeans back on. I crawl over to Seven, but suddenly I can't look at him. It's somehow easier with our captor. Despite his mocking and taunts, I know he doesn't judge me because he doesn't judge. There isn't some moral barometer inside his brain deciding this is okay and that is not. So nothing I can do will ever earn judgment from him. It may earn me punishment, but never judgment.

Seven is different. He might judge me, even if he doesn't want to. And I find myself resenting him a little for it. But then my gaze is drawn to the evidence of his desire. He is so hard, his erection bulging behind his pants, straining to be free to get inside my mouth, to get to the warm wet pleasure he's just been promised.

Our captor stands just behind me, his fingers tangling in my hair. "I want to watch him come down your throat, Pretty Toy. I want to watch you swallow like a good obedient whore."

I am so turned on right now. I know I shouldn't be. I'm in too much danger to let myself fall into this fucked-up seduction. And it's even more fucked-up that my brain conjures up the word *seduction* in relation to anything that's going on right now.

He removes his hand from my hair, and I turn back to Seven. I struggle with the button and zipper on his jeans to free him. When his cock springs free, I'm about to open my mouth to take him, when a glint of something shiny catches my eye. The syringe lies on the ground, outside of Seven's reach, but not outside mine.

I chance a quick glance up at him, and his eyes widen a fraction as he realizes what I just saw. I know our captor will kill us eventually, and I don't want to die.

Before I can let myself think or lose my courage, I grab the syringe, spin around, and jab it into our captor's thigh. I push the plunger down, making sure all the drug has emptied into his bloodstream.

I look up to find his eyes widen as he stumbles to the ground.

"Get the key," Seven says. As if he needed to say that.

When I'm sure our captor is completely out, I slide my hand down inside his front pocket where I saw him deposit the key. It takes actual willpower not to ogle his bare chest. I'm trying to escape this psycho and somehow still feel the need to stop and admire the scenery. The animal part of me that only cares about rutting with a strong alpha male doesn't care about the reality of the situation or why I need to flee, not mount him. But he left me wanting, and the ache between my legs hasn't died down just because an opportunity to get away presented itself.

Finally I turn back toward Seven. "You'll have to drag him over to the door and stretch his arm up to the panel so we can use his thumbprint to get out," I say, which truthfully is probably as obvious as his *Get the key* comment. But too much adrenaline is flowing to think through all the things which must be obvious to both of us in this critical moment.

I know our captor will probably be out for a while, but I'm still shaking so hard, rushing to try to unlock the metal cuff around Seven's wrist. I still can barely comprehend our luck.

"You're doing great," Seven says.

It takes several attempts before I'm able to successfully insert the key into the lock and turn it, freeing one of his arms. I hand him the key because I don't think I can manage the next one on my own. He takes it from my shaking hand to unlock his other wrist.

I hear movement and turn, horrified, to find our captor

standing over me. "Oh, Pretty Toy, that was an unfortunate choice."

I turn quickly back to Seven to find he's gotten his other wrist free. He pulls himself to stand, but before he can prepare to fight off our captor, a needle is going into his neck, and he slumps to the floor. Does it just last a few minutes?

Our captor has the shackles around Seven's wrists and the key back in his pocket faster than I can process.

I scramble back as he advances. He tips the syringe he just injected into Seven toward me to reveal a red round label on top of the plunger.

"This is the one with the drugs. What you gave me? Was a saline solution. It was a test, and I'm sorry to say you failed it, Kate."

I look over to Seven's unconscious body then back to our captor. I don't think people can really die from fear. Because if they could, I would be dead right now—a shadowy misty soul floating high in the air above my expired corpse. But no, fate is not so kind to give me such a quick death, and the look in his eyes says whatever is coming will be slow.

He just shakes his head at me, looking disappointed. The sickest part of this moment is the fact that there's a part of me that feels... contrite. As though I did something wrong. As though I broke his trust. *His* trust. Maybe it's better if he just kills me because I'm already too aberrant to live. I don't want to see the woman I will become if he keeps letting me breathe.

Broken sobs slip out of me even as I try to keep them locked down.

"Not going to beg me? Or was that just for when you were pretending to be a good girl?"

"Would it do any good?" I ask, already knowing the answer.

"No." Gone is his sarcastic word play and his amused expressions as he reveals each new twist in his game.

He sighs, "Come with me, Pretty Toy."

I don't move. What difference does it make if I try to obey him now or if I resist? "Are you going to kill me?"

"No, Kate." He stretches out his hand. He's far calmer than I would expect. I did jab a needle with what I thought were drugs in his leg after all. "Now," he says.

I want him to rush at me, all anger and venom. I want him to grab me and forcibly remove me from the room, drag me kicking and screaming to the dungeon because I cannot just voluntarily walk toward him. But he doesn't. He just waits.

He can apparently wait forever for me to go to him. What else can I do? Run? Where? Around the cell? Into the bathroom? There's nowhere to hide, no way to escape. He can just let me wear myself out.

"It will be worse for you if you don't come with me now."

These words are all I need to start moving, this small permission to obey him without self-recrimination. After all, it will be *worse* if I don't. So I'm not the stupid girl walking willingly to her doom. I'm the smart girl, stopping this from escalating and becoming *worse*.

I take the offered hand and he leads me over to the door. There's a brief pause while he presses his thumb against the thumbprint scanner, and the door slides open, taking us back out into that impossibly ornate hallway.

"Are you hungry?" he asks.

I hadn't noticed it with everything that has transpired. "Yes, Master."

I expect he will lead me to the end of the hallway and that other steel door that leads into the underground dungeon, but he doesn't. Instead, we stop a couple of doors before that where he takes me into a large modern kitchen.

"Sit," he says, indicating a bar near the kitchen island.

I sit on a stool, bewildered.

"I'm going to say this once, Kate. This house is locked down. There's no way out. Every window is locked and can only be opened with a key. Each door is locked. The windows are shatterproof. There's an alarm that would sound anyway if anything was breached. So don't be stupid again."

I watch quietly as he takes out some pans and begins to make bacon and eggs. I don't understand what's happening. I thought he was going to kill me, but he claims he isn't. And I'm sure he'll punish me. The fact that he's decided he wants to *feed* me right now is beyond my comprehension.

I feel suddenly self-conscious being naked upstairs in his bright kitchen with black and white parquet floors and the huge windows which offer me a stunning view of the gently rolling landscape outside.

My gaze shifts to a wooden block with an array of no doubt very sharp kitchen knives in it. He turns away from the stove and catches my guilty gaze.

He chuckles. "Don't even think about it. You don't want to escalate our relationship to knives. Trust me."

I swallow hard and nod. Even as the smell of bacon and eggs wafts to my nose, I'm losing my appetite. How can I possibly eat knowing something extremely bad is about to happen to me? I try to keep my tears quiet, but I fail.

He makes no comment.

When the food is done, he places it in front of me and pours me a glass of milk. "Eat."

I'm not sure if it's the smell of the food triggering my appetite or if somehow biologically my body now responds to his commands. I think it's the first thing but I wouldn't swear on it.

"Aren't *you* going to eat?" I ask.

"I already ate."

He cleans up the kitchen and washes the dishes, then he leans against the kitchen island, watching me as I finish up the last bite of eggs. He takes the plate and glass from me and washes those as well. I pray it takes him forever to finish this task so I can stay in the warm, bright, safe kitchen a little longer. At the same time, I can't stand the maddeningly slow way he moves, the way he drags out the time leading to whatever horrors await me for stabbing him with a needle while trying to escape. Can he really blame me for wanting to be free and safe?

"Come, Pretty Toy," he says.

Then he just walks out of the kitchen. He doesn't grab me and drag me along like some hostage. He simply expects that I will get up and follow him. And I will because every door and window is locked. Everything is shatterproof. There's an alarm. Resisting or running is pointless, and it will only make him angry. I bite back another sob as I slide off the kitchen bar stool and follow him out of the room and the rest of the way down the hallway to that steel door with the security panel that leads down to hell.

He inputs a code, and the door slides open. There's a wide, sweeping motion of his arm in that gallant *after you* gesture. I'm sure I'm about to faint. A wave of dizziness moves over me, and my legs don't want to support my body anymore, but I take a deep breath, and it passes.

He waits.

I feel the tears sliding down my cheeks again. But I know they don't move him—at least not in the way I would want them to. The outline of his erection pressing against the fabric of his jeans tells me that much. I walk in front of him, down the winding stairs into the dungeon.

I'm already on my knees when he gets down there, mostly because I can't hold myself up. And really, it's more like child's pose in yoga. I need to breathe, and this is the only way I can get deep enough breaths into my body without hyperventilating. It's only a bonus that I know it will please him and look like submission. Maybe it is submission. I know it's fear.

His footsteps stop next to me, and then he sits on the ground. I flinch when he strokes my hair and then my back. Over and over again. This is the last thing I expected from him after what happened upstairs—gentleness. And I know it's a lie, but I don't care. I will drink it up like it's the last drop of water on earth. I need just another few minutes of peace before he hurts me.

Oh god, what is he going to do to me?

"I'm not going to harm you," he finally says.

"But I thought..." I shut my mouth because what the fuck am I doing? If he's decided not to hurt me, I don't want to argue him out of it. *Be smarter, Kate.*

"I'm going to train you. Don't misunderstand. This isn't kindness or a long lost conscience rearing its head. It's just the best choice for the outcome I want. Punishment and pain are always an option. And I'll use them as necessary, but I want to own every part of you. Completely. If I use too much pain, your fear will drive you to try to escape again. I would never truly own you. But if I inspire gratitude... you're mine forever."

Well, at least he's laid out his evil plan, so I don't have to drive myself crazy trying to figure out what's going on. Even as I think these thoughts, I know he's calculated the choice of even telling me this. And already I feel gratitude moving through me, unbidden. When one goes from thinking they're going to die to thinking they're going to be tortured, to a good breakfast and the absence of those things... gratitude is the only response one is capable of.

I know I shouldn't feel it. He's keeping me as a slave. He took me away from my life—such that it was. None of this is okay, but I feel so grateful anyway as if everything he's done so far has been one giant favor. And the pleasure and desire that repeatedly winds its way through me at his touch and the promise of it makes it seem true.

The words, "Thank you, Master," slip out of me so fast I can't stop them.

He chuckles at this. He has me exactly where he wants me. I think he *wanted* me to jab that needle into him no matter what he says about his disappointment at me failing his *test*. He's not disappointed. It's all going according to plan.

Even if I had experience with psychopaths, it wouldn't matter. I'm one hundred percent sure that there's not another human alive who would make the choices this man makes. He possesses the most terrifying combination of brilliance, evil, and patience. And I'm the unlucky lottery winner of his attentions.

"Why are you doing this to me?" I whisper.

"That question was a long time coming. Because I want to."

There's a long silence. He finally speaks again. "Were you expecting a sad childhood story? Did you want to understand what turned me into such a soulless beast? Would that make it all okay? If you could point to some moment in time where I was a sad, scared little boy? Well, sorry to disappoint, Pretty Toy. That's not my story. My parents gave me everything I could ever want. I started out having everything, and then I doubled that wealth. I've acquired every object I've ever wanted, and now I've acquired you. My living, breathing fuck doll."

He stands, then I feel his hands wrapped around mine, helping me off the floor. He leads me to the bondage bed at the far end of the dungeon and lays me down on my back. I watch as he goes to the large box where he got the vibrator the last time. He returns with a ball gag.

"Open," he says when he's beside me.

I open my mouth, and he presses the black rubber ball into place, fastening the straps behind my head. Then he presses a button on a remote, and the classical music I'd almost forgotten about begins to fill the dungeon. It's all so... civilized.

He doesn't restrain me. On a certain level, it's overkill. He doesn't need to tie me down unless it pleases him. The door at the top of the stairs is locked. There's no way out. I could jump off the bed and try to run, but he might change his mind about punishment if I do that. And I would eventually get tired. He only has to wait me out. He's already shown how patient and willing to wait he is.

The gag is worse than the restraints. With restraints, I can still beg. Even though I know there's nothing human in him, it still seems to amuse him and please him enough to offer me small indulgences. But I don't even have the power to beg now.

I watch warily as he lies beside me. He props himself on his side and observes me. I look away from his cold gray stare. It's too much to have that gaze leveled on me, taking me in, analyzing, deciding my fate.

"Look at me, Pretty Toy," he says. There's a warning wrapped inside the command.

I take a breath and look back at him, trying to hold his gaze. I flinch when he brushes my hair out of my eyes. Then he spends a small eternity just stroking my breasts and watching my reactions. He massages them first gently, then more roughly. He pinches my nipples into hard points and then releases the pressure.

Eventually, the tension eases from my body. I become soft and yielding. I find myself pressing into his hand, moaning behind the gag, my eyes drifting closed as my body arches into each caress.

"Good girl," he murmurs.

These words unlock the need between my legs as the arousal pulses to life again.

"If I put my fingers inside your pussy, will you be wet for me?"

I nod.

His hand trails over my belly and between my legs. I can hear my wetness as he presses a finger inside me. He smiles, satisfied with my body's response.

"This is mine. And because I allow it, Seven's. You're going to be our good whore. No more silly escape attempts. No more denying your desires. You want this, don't you, Pretty Toy?"

I could lie to myself. I could say that I only nod in answer to appease him, to try to stay safe. But I do have needs. I'm only human, and they are both so beautiful. There's no resistance to Seven. But our captor? I wish it was somehow okay to want what he's doing right now, to just exist and float on this haze of erotic satisfaction.

I'm supposed to fight. I'm supposed to struggle and cry and beg him not to touch me. But I just open my legs wider, holding his gaze, arching up to meet his fingers as they slide in and out of me.

"You will give me your pleasure. It belongs to me. The first thing you need to learn is how to come for me."

I'm pretty sure I already know how to do that. I feel myself blush at the memory of what he did that first day on this bed.

He chuckles. "No, I mean you're going to learn how to come *for* me. You're going to come, and then come again, and then again, until *I* say it's time to stop. Sometimes pleasure can be so much that it becomes pain. You'll learn that, and then you'll learn to accept it and push through it to give me more of your pleasure. Until I allow you to stop."

My eyes widen at this. I'm not that woman who has multiple orgasms. I don't know that I can't, I've just never tried. I'm satisfied after one. Again I find myself wondering what happens if I can't give him what he wants. A punishment of some type? I'm growing less afraid that he'll kill me. My escape attempt didn't push him to it so I now feel irrationally safe from death—at least for the foreseeable future. I'm not sure how accurate this assessment is, but it makes me feel the tiniest bit less guilty for the way I crave his touch.

He gets up and stretches my arms and legs out and binds me to the bed, much like he had me that first day. He produces a blindfold from a drawer in the base of the bed and secures it around my eyes.

I feel the panic edging in. Bound, no sight, no ability to cry out.

"Shhhh," he says, stroking the side of my face. "I will remove the gag on one condition. You're not allowed to beg. You can make any sounds you want but no words. Do you accept these terms?"

I nod, desperate to have even the tiniest freedom.

"I want to be sure you understand. If you beg me, if you say a single word to me that I don't command, you will be punished. I can leave the gag in. It won't be comfortable, but you'll be safe. Do you want me to leave it in?"

I shake my head.

He sighs. "All right. Be careful with this favor, Pretty Toy. It may bite you in the end."

This scares me a little. *Can* I resist the urge to beg? To try to reason with him? To speak the title he's demanded from me over and over?

I don't know, but the gag is starting to hurt, and it makes me panic and feel like I can't take in proper breaths. He unfastens the straps and pulls it off me. I lick my dry lips, then something plastic prods at my mouth.

"Drink." When I hesitate, he says "It's only water."

I take the water he offers, then lie back when he pulls it away.

A moment later, I feel his tongue between my legs, and I'm already past the point of even pretending to resist him. I don't speak. I don't beg. I just arch up toward his exploring tongue, whimpers and moans flowing out of me.

My first orgasm comes after only a few minutes. But he doesn't stop. He drinks me up, never slowing in his assault on my senses. He pulls away, and I'm panting.

He leaves me for a moment, and I take a long shaky breath. I know he isn't finished with me. Upon his return, I hear the distinct buzzing sound. I can tell he has it on the highest setting.

I cringe away before he reaches me, but he spreads me wide so that he can press these intense vibrations directly against my clit. I struggle away from the sensation, but there's nowhere to go. He grips my hip, stilling me.

"Be good and accept it, Pretty Toy."

I breathe slowly. After a little while, the sensations start to feel like pleasure again as another orgasm prepares to crest over me. But before it can, he pulls it away from my clit.

The words "Please, Master" are at the edge of my

tongue before I bite them back, remembering the promise of punishment.

He chuckles at this. He pushes the vibrator inside me much as he did that first day. This time I know I'll come. And it's as earthshattering as it was the first time, building from some place deep within me and then exploding outward. I buck my hips with it, trying to fuck the toy instead of the toy fucking me.

I'm panting and whimpering when it finally subsides, and he pulls the toy away. But he only allows me a minute of rest before he's started in on me again. He uses multiple toys in a rotation as he drags orgasm out of orgasm from my quivering pussy.

My legs shake with the force of each release, and I bite my tongue to stop myself from begging please, no more. Please, please, Master, stop. But I hold these words in. I don't want to be punished. But in its own way, this is becoming a different kind of punishment.

Still, I don't allow myself to beg.

Some of the toys vibrate, some of them don't. One feels similar to oral sex against my clit. Some are larger than others, stretching me as they make me come for him. Sometimes he stimulates my clit, and other times he brings my orgasm out from the inside, training me to produce these new and exciting pleasurable pulses at his command.

I've lost count of how many orgasms I've had.

The next thing that slides inside me is his cock. He's on top of me, his movements so achingly slow that even with all the pleasure I've already had, I find myself arching up into him.

He leans close to my ear. "This time, you will come."

I've come so many times since we've been down here that it's nothing to my body to do it just one more time for his cock. He shudders and releases inside me as my pussy grips onto him, milking him while riding out my own orgasm.

Finally, he collapses on top of me. And then he's peppering kisses over my throat, moving to my mouth, causing me to jump as his tongue slips inside. His kiss is consuming, possessing. I didn't expect him to kiss me, and I'm so confused by how it makes me feel.

After a few more minutes, I hear him collecting and moving things about. Water runs in an attached room, probably a bathroom, as he cleans things up. He returns and unties me but leaves the blindfold in place. I feel unsteady as he helps me to stand.

"Come with me," he says. He guides me slowly across the floor and up the stairs. When we leave the dungeon I sense we're moving back down that same hallway.

I think he's returning me to the cell, but there's a shift in direction. Then we're climbing another set of stairs. Another hallway. After what just happened in the dungeon, I feel so tired, I'm afraid I'll collapse. But before I can, he picks me up and lays me down on a bed.

He locks a chain around my ankle and removes the blindfold. He covers me with blankets. I'm dimly aware that he's brought me up to what must be his room.

"Sleep."

He pulls the shades down and turns out the light, then leaves me alone in his bed. I haven't been awake that long, but after all that happened this morning, I'm so exhausted that it doesn't take very long for sleep to claim me.

Several days pass, and a routine is formed. I sleep in my captor's bed with him each night. He fondles me. He fucks me. He lies behind me and wraps his arm around my waist, pulling me into him—the little spoon—as though we're normal lovers. As though I mean something to him. This intimate cuddling is what unmakes me the most; it's the thing that makes it harder and harder to think of escape.

He's trained me to wake him with a blow job each morning and to swallow like a good girl. When I complete this task, he rewards me with those words which fill me with an inappropriate pride each time I hear them. After that, he feeds me, bathes me, and then takes me to the dungeon where he forces orgasm after orgasm out of me until he's satisfied.

It's easier to please him with blow jobs. In the dungeon, he never seems to want to allow my body rest. It's his fingers, his tongue, the vibrator, his cock. Over and over until I've lost track of the orgasms. And I'm supposed to count them. When I forget to count or lose track of how many, he punishes me.

His punishments hurt but haven't been overly harsh. I've never felt I was in true physical danger from them.

And every day he spends a lot of time on my ass. First it was his finger, lubed, pressing into me. I squirmed away at first, terrified, but he petted my hair and spoke soft words and was so gentle that I let my body relax until it did feel good. Strange, but also somehow pleasurable.

Since then he's been working me up with toys and butt plugs, slowly stretching me. I know what he's preparing me for, and a dark part of me is excited.

There's a strange comfort in this routine, much like the one I'd formed with Seven for those few days when he touched me in the dark at night.

I'm worried about Seven. Is he alive? Is he hurt? Is he being neglected? Is he being fed? I wish I knew what was happening to him. Does our captor feed him when he's not with me? I've been afraid to ask. He hasn't given any indication he doesn't still want to share me, so maybe that guarantees Seven's safety and continuing existence.

Today after our daily routine, he takes me to a small room with large screens along the wall, revealing different angles of the cell Seven is in.

"Sit," he orders.

I sit in the rolling leather chair, and he binds my wrists to the arms using cable ties from a desk nearby.

"Stay. And watch that screen." I couldn't disobey the first order, unless I got out of the room and rolled down the hallway.

Before I can respond, he's gone. I turn my gaze back to the screen. Seven is chained in the cell. He can't have been chained the entire time because he looks clean, and the cell is clean. He's obviously used the bathroom and shower facilities. So that means our captor must be drugging him multiple times a day. This thought upsets me.

You can't just keep someone drugged like that without causing serious health consequences. Our captor never drugs me, but what happens when Seven starts to get sick from all the drugs building up in his system?

I'm relieved at least to see he's still alive. If he was beaten again, I can't find evidence of it. But his back is against the wall, so I can't know for sure. I tense as I watch the metal door slide open in the cell. Our captor pushes in a giant screen on wheels. From one of the screens in the control room I can see Seven clearly head on. From another I can see the screen that has been rolled into the cell.

"Where is she?" Seven demands. "Is she alive? If you've hurt her..."

"Relax, Hero. She's alive. She's fine. No permanent marks anywhere but her soul. She's still with me, learning to be good. Don't worry, I'll share her with you again soon. You still have to be trained to take proper control of her."

Seven says nothing in response to this, but his glare tells me everything. I wish I could reach the microphone and the button on the control panel to talk to him and let him know I'm okay.

"I have a treat for you," our captor says. "I felt bad that you weren't there for that first day when I took her into the dungeon. You missed watching the way she surrendered so sweetly to me. But I made a video. Would you like to see it?"

"No," he says flatly, but he can't hide the curiosity and desire in his eyes.

Our captor laughs. "Yes, you do. Don't worry. I won't tell her you watched." He pushes a play button on the screen and leaves Seven alone in the cell.

I'm horrified to see myself as he spanks me while I beg then asks if I want pleasure or pain. I don't want to watch myself like this, but I am riveted by the erotic display in front of me, so much so that I've forgotten Seven altogether.

Several minutes pass as I watch the kind of porn men would pay for. I jump when I hear the door to the control room open, and he's with me again.

"Wrong screen, Pretty Toy. Watch Seven."

I turn my gaze to the other screen, shocked to find Seven's cock freed of his jeans as he watches and jerks off to the images in front of him.

My master leans close to my ear. "See, Kate, we're all the same. He's no better than me. He's sitting there, getting off knowing you were terrified and tied up at my mercy. He's getting off watching me make you come. And he does this, even without knowing what I've been doing to you the last week. If I've starved you, if I've beaten you. He just can't help himself. We're all animals in the end."

His hand moves between my legs, and he chuckles. "I've trained you so well. So fucking wet. Are you ready to go back to Seven? I think it's time we both fucked you, don't you? Admit it, you want us both inside you."

I strain for more contact, trying to grind my clit against his hand, but he pulls away. "Save it for Seven."

I turn back to the screen in time to see Seven come on the concrete floor with a satisfied groan as if he's been saving it up the entire time I've been away from him.

Our captor flicks a switch on the control panel and leans into the microphone. "Kate is here with me, watching you come like a horny teenager. But I kept my word; I didn't *tell* her you were watching."

Seven's hand stills on his cock. When he looks up at the screen, he looks guilty.

"I'm bringing her back to you now, so you'll be able to offer your sincerest apologies. I'm sure she'll be moved."

WHEN I'M RETURNED TO THE CELL, SEVEN CAN'T MEET MY gaze. I run, flinging myself into his arms. He holds tightly onto me, clearly surprised that I'm not hurt or angry, pushing him away after what I just saw him do. I bury my head in his chest, breathing in his clean masculine scent, feeling his heartbeat thud against my own skin.

I expect our captor to stay, but he leaves us alone in the cell. A minute later, I hear a metallic sound as the silver key drops through the slot again. I go get it and unlock Seven's wrists. This time I'm shaking because I've missed him so much and just want to get the damn chains off him.

When he's finally free, he stands and pulls me into his arms for a real hug.

"Are you okay, Kitten?"

"Yes, Master."

He doesn't flinch when I say it this time. After he just jerked off to a video of me helplessly coming for our captor, this title I offer him no longer seems like such a big deal.

He doesn't ask any more questions about what happened to me. I know he doesn't want to know, and I don't want to tell it. The main reason I don't want to tell it is because what happened to me wasn't nearly as terrible as I wish I could say it was.

We soak together in the tub, and he takes me again in the shower. At night, we lie in the darkness, and he resumes his pattern of stroking me to orgasm, my moan filling the cell before we both drift off to sleep wrapped in each other's arms.

This temporary peace is broken the next morning.

"Breakfast time, inmates," our captor says cheerily over the speaker.

Seven goes to the slot to collect the food. It's sausage and gravy biscuits. A white plate and a blue plate. I know what this means even before our captor's voice rings out again.

"The blue plate special is for Seven."

"You can't keep drugging him like this," I say. "You'll kill him."

Our captor laughs. "Awwww, Seven has a girlfriend. So sweet. He'll be fine. He's tough."

A couple of water bottles are dropped in through the slot.

We sit on the floor of the cell and eat in silence. Seven goes to sit against the wall when he's finished. After a few minutes, he's unconscious.

I move back to my corner when the door slides open and warily watch our captor. He drags Seven to the door.

"Don't hurt him," I say.

"Careful, Pretty Toy. I might get jealous of the affection you lavish on him."

I don't say anything else. Afraid that if I do, he might take it out on Seven. He presses his thumb against the scanner and takes Seven out of the cell.

He returns a couple of hours later, and I'm terrified by what he may have done to Seven in that time and why he hasn't brought him back.

"Come," he says, beckoning me toward him. I slowly get up off the floor and walk even more slowly. Even just a few hours away from our routine, and his constant attentions has made me afraid again.

"It's okay. I'm not going to hurt you."

He opens the door and urges me out ahead of him. His hand rests on my bare lower back as he guides me down the hallway to the door that leads down to the dungeon. He strokes my back when I tense.

"It's okay," he says again as he inputs the code.

When we get downstairs, Seven is still unconscious, lying naked on his back, spread-eagled and bound to the bed the same way I've so often been. It's hard to look at him like this and imagine this was what I looked like. So exposed and vulnerable.

I rush to him, running my hands over his body, searching for injuries, but unless it's his back, I don't see anything. But there must be something.

"What did you do to him?" I demand.

He advances on me and pulls me off Seven before

pushing me up against the wall, his hand at my throat, his gray gaze holding mine. "Do *not* speak to me in that disrespectful tone."

I'm crying and struggling even though he isn't squeezing hard.

"I'm sorry... M-master. Please. Please."

He releases me and takes a step back, straightening his clothes as if he's civilized and above these petty threats. "Now, to answer your question, I've done nothing to him. The drugs were for transport, and it takes a while for them to wear off. I haven't touched him."

I hear a groan and turn toward the bed where Seven is waking up. "Let me go, motherfucker!" he growls.

"Ah, ah... There's a lady present," our captor says.

Seven turns sharply toward me. "Ka—" He stops himself in time. "Kitten," he says instead.

"Okay," our captor says, a delighted gleam in his eyes. "I just thought up a fun game. Last time it was lady's choice. Let's switch it up. Seven... you get to choose. Do I punish Kate or does she give me a blow job?"

I freeze at this and look at Seven. His expression mirrors my own.

"If it helps, whichever one you pick, you get to watch. And Kate, you can't tell him which you prefer. It takes all the fun out."

The truth is, he's twisted me so much in just a few days alone with him that I would be okay with either, but only if the punishment was like other punishments—not so much I can't stand it. But I'm afraid if Seven chooses for me to be punished, our captor will go harder on me to punish *him*. I'm afraid he'll make me bleed.

I know Seven; even though he's seen how I respond to our captor, he won't want to choose to put me in a sexual situation I might not want. It's a wasted worry on his part. I'm already too far gone, but I don't know how to communicate this with just my eyes. And the truth is, I'm ashamed to, because there's something about the idea that I would rather suck our captor's cock while Seven watches than take a punishment that seems too twisted to accept.

"Punish me," Seven says.

"No. That's not the choice. You always try to cheat the rules."

"I'm not choosing either thing," Seven spits out, glaring at our captor.

A sigh. "This is so tiring. Have I not already established how everything works? I say do something, you refuse, I withhold food, you do it, you get fed. Why not skip the suffering part? It's not as though I get some pleasure out of not feeding bad pets."

"I can't *choose* to hurt her!" Seven roars.

"Then choose the blow job."

"That's hurting her!"

Our captor laughs. "Oh, sweet, innocent Seven. Where *did* you come from? She's practically salivating at the idea of being on her knees with my cock in her mouth while you watch and get hard."

Seven looks at me, and I look away, but I know my face is red, revealing the truth of that sick statement.

"I'm not choosing to hurt her," Seven says more quietly.

"I've had blow jobs all week, and she was perfectly eager. She's less eager about pain. It's an easy choice."

"No," Seven says.

"Fine. I'll leave you two down here a couple of days, and you can decide when I come back."

I touch Seven's arm. "Master, please. Whatever you choose is okay."

It's not really. I don't want to be punished. I know what our captor wants, and if Seven gives him any other answer, he'll take it out on me even harder. But I also know by now that if I tell him what to choose, I'll be punished for that, too. It may have taken a while, but I'm getting smarter about how to play his games. I may not be able to win, but at least I can avoid losing.

"Okay, I'm bored." Our captor turns to go back up the stairs.

"No, please!" I say.

"Blow job," Seven says quietly.

I let out a sigh of relief.

"Excellent!" our captor says. He moves to sit in a chair a few feet away from the bed right in Seven's line of sight. He unzips his pants and crooks a finger, smug satisfaction painted across his face. And god help me, but his power has started to corrode something inside me and turn me on. His smug arrogance is no barrier to the wetness gathering between my thighs.

"Crawl to me, Pretty Toy."

I drop to my hands and knees and crawl across the floor, the thrumming excitement between my legs only growing in anticipation. Part of me wants to hide how aroused I am from Seven, but then I realize it will hurt him less if he knows that I'm not being *hurt* by this.

So I don't hold back.

When I reach him, I spend a few moments dragging

my tongue over his cock as though I have all day and he is my favorite type of candy, which I want to make last forever. He chuckles at this but indulges my languid exploration. I know all the places he's most sensitive, and I lick and kiss and gently suck until I feel the power between us shift the slightest amount, if for only a moment as he groans with the need for more.

His fingers thread into my hair, guiding but not forcing. It's the most surprising and wonderful thing I've learned about him the last few days. Although he's large, he never tries to choke or gag me with his cock. He doesn't fuck my mouth like some animal. Oral sex is the only time with him where I feel like I have the power. I know I only have it because he allows it, but still, it makes everything between us feel different. It has made it harder and harder to see myself as his captive, even though I'm kept chained beside his bed or in the cell with Seven.

Sometimes I swear he'll say *Please* if I tease him for too long. But he never does even though I can feel the word screaming out in his mind.

The teasing now leaves no doubt for Seven that I'm not actually suffering through this. I *want* to be here. No matter what it says about me, I like being on my knees in front of him like this, wrapping my mouth around his cock. I devote myself completely to the task now, taking him further down my throat. I relax and let him inside as far as I can take.

I can't take it all, but he doesn't force it all. I know exactly where the pleasure gathers in him, where to focus my attentions. After a few minutes of greater dedication, he comes.

My throat works to swallow as he tries to regain the capacity for speech. When he finally succeeds, the words he speaks goes straight to my core.

"That's right, my sweet whore, take it all. Such a good girl."

He strokes my throat as I swallow. When I'm finished and pull away from him, he absently strokes my hair, guiding me to rest my head against his thigh. I hate how much I love this affection from him.

I hate how I feel like a puppy, proud of performing a trick properly. And I hate how badly I want him to fuck me right now.

Or maybe this is all a lie. Maybe I don't hate any of these things no matter how much I know I should.

"Look at him. Look how hard he is."

I raise my head up and turn to find Seven fully erect.

"Get on the bed with him."

He doesn't need to ask twice. I crawl onto the bed and lie down next to Seven. I rest my head against the center of his chest, my hand drifting down over his stomach until I find his cock. It jumps against my touch as I stroke it.

"We're going to take her together. At the same time. I'd let you take her ass, but I can't trust you to unchain you. I gave this a lot of thought actually, but I know how it would play out. You'd try to fight me, even though you'd be locked down here without the code. Then, if you bested me, you'd tie me up and then do whatever was necessary—assuming you aren't all talk and could stomach it—until I cracked and gave you the code. So we have to do it this way."

This villain monologue doesn't do anything to dampen Seven's desire. He's seen too much to push it away now. I don't even think he'll object to the idea of them both fucking me together. Even though I'm sure he's afraid it will hurt me. How could he know our captor has been preparing my body patiently for days so I can take this?

I run my fingertips gently along Seven's stomach. His body is strung so tight with tension. I press a kiss against his chest and up to his neck. The tension slowly starts to drain out, but he's fighting to hold onto it.

He can't let himself enjoy this because he hasn't been broken the way I have—with pleasure.

"Now, Pretty Toy... I want you to get on your hands and knees so that you're straddling his body, and keep eye contact. But I don't want you to fuck yet. You can have him inside you when I *say* you can have him inside you."

I can't stop the whimper as I move to obey his command. The last time in the cell, as I was grabbing the syringe, there was the smallest twisted regret that I wouldn't get to have them both. It had simmered beneath the surface, a thought I couldn't allow to take full form, but it was there. Now that I've seen the futility of escape, I'm grateful for a second chance to do this.

I now live in our captor's darkness. I breathe it like oxygen. As the rest of reality has faded away, the only thing that remains is pleasure and desire. The question on my mind is no longer *how can I escape him?* It's *how can I climb the mountain to reach the peak of my orgasm faster? How can I come harder?* Though our captor never leaves me to solve these complex problems on my own. He's a fixer.

A moment later, he's behind me, pushing a lubed toy slowly in and out of my ass. It's a little smaller than he is, but not by much. I hold Seven's gaze and moan as I adjust to the toy and begin to crave more. But Seven isn't yet in this. He still feels the guilt. He can't give himself over. So I lean forward and kiss him.

His mouth opens to accept my tongue, and a moment later, I feel him truly join me. If he was free to do so, he'd wrap his arms around me and pull me so far into him no one would be able to detect where one of us ends and the other begins.

I yelp and pull away as a hard slap connects with my ass.

"Eye contact, Kate."

"I'm sorry, Master."

I hold Seven's gaze in mine while our captor prepares me. He takes his time as he recovers from his last release. Finally, he says, "Mount him like a bitch in heat and ride."

I moan just at that order. I wish this man hadn't taken me captive and that I could give myself over completely to him. No matter how much I know that morality no longer matters for us, I can't change my emotional nature and make it okay to give this man my soul. And I know it's not safe.

So I shift this energy to Seven as I lower myself on top of him. A tiny cry leaves my throat as I let him fully inside. My greedy pussy grabs hold of him as though his cock is the last thing that will ever fill me. And then I begin to move.

It isn't long before our captor has removed the toy. Now it's his slickly lubed cock easing inside me with so much more gentleness than a man like him should be capable of or even care to offer. I'm filled with and overwhelmed by both men now. One darkness, the other light. Both of them go still, as I adjust.

I move first.

I ride Seven as our captor rides me. He strokes my breasts, pinching my nipple so hard I scream, but it isn't from the pain. It's from the pleasure that just intensified between my legs. I'm so wet I can hear myself as I move on Seven's cock. His intense hazel gaze is locked on mine.

Our captor doesn't even have to touch my clit. I've been trained so well to respond that all I need is something inside me now, and the way they both feel moving together is so intense that my orgasm catches me off guard. And now, for the first time, I come with Seven inside me. And I am loud. And I don't care. All I care about is that I'm in the midst of the most powerfully transcendent sexual release of my life.

The two of them come with their own more masculine, guttural sounds a moment later. And now... we are all in this together.

8

It feels like I've existed in this cell forever. I should have been counting the days more closely, but they all bleed together. And why does it matter how long this has gone on?

I wake to find Seven asleep on the floor. I shake him to try to wake him and realize it's not normal sleep. Did our captor slip in and dose him again? He never drugs me. He doesn't need to. I'm so small and weak, I can't put up a real struggle, but Seven is his match. He may even be a bit stronger than our captor, so more precautions must be taken.

Though our captor plays with us and watches us fuck each other, he still hasn't fully broken Seven. I know his eventual plan is for Seven to fully embrace this role as my master, so that our captor can let him off the leash. He's tempted him. He's promised him he doesn't have to stay in the cell. There are much nicer rooms upstairs. They can be on the same side. I can be their captive together. But Seven refuses to take any of the bait on offer.

Our captor will never be able to trust Seven unchained. He's not a dog that can be trained. I somehow have grown to think of him as my protector, even though he can't truly protect me from anything. Not like this. The door opens, and I scoot back to the far corner of the cell. As much as he has taken me and shaped me to his will, as much as my body wants him, there's the lingering uncertainty, the fear that the mask of calm will drop and this will all end.

He chains Seven up, then smacks him a few times in the face.

"Wake up!"

Seven slowly comes to. His eyes immediately find mine as if reassuring himself I'm still here and okay. It does something to me when he looks at me like this.

"Good. I need you both awake for this announcement," our captor says.

I want to join Seven. I want to be wrapped in his arms right now, but our captor is standing beside him, and I don't dare make that trip across the cell because something has changed, and I'm terrified that I think I know what it is.

I've craved both of these men, but it only feels right or sane with Seven, so I pour all my emotional energy into him and try to forget the excitement I feel when the other man touches me. Obviously, it's Stockholm Syndrome, but even so, it's convincingly real. It's reminds me of a lucid dream I once had where I spent several minutes just touching this textured wallpaper, knowing I was dreaming but unable to comprehend how real it all felt. As I'd stroked the velvety smooth wall, I kept thinking to myself *how can this not be real?*

This dream is even more real.

"I've grown tired of this game," our captor says.

The tears come immediately. It's like I've locked them away and saved them just for this moment. He's going to kill us. I knew this day was coming, but I'd hoped it would be farther in the future. I crawl over to him, forgetting my former resistance. "Please, Master... don't..." But I can't bring myself to say the words. If he's grown tired of this game, there's nothing I can do to change his mind. I've always known I existed at his pleasure, on his terms.

I flinch when he strokes my hair. He sighs. "I'm going to let you go," he says finally.

"W-what?" I can't have heard him right. He can't just let us go. How would that even work? Isn't he afraid we'll report him? Before I can work through all the ramifications and how he could possibly let us go without endangering himself, the reality that I've spent weeks ignoring because it no longer mattered, slaps me in the face.

I still have no job, no money, no apartment. Probably not even clothes. I'm sure Carolyn must have tossed my things when I didn't come back for them. I will starve to death out there. I'm pretty sure I can't get Andrew to take me back, not after he thinks I stood him up that night and just never spoke to him again.

He probably thinks I was fucking around with him somehow. And after what has happened here in this cell, I don't think I could ever...

"Master, please... I'll starve. I have nothing, I can't..." I can't believe I'm saying this. But this is truly the situation

I'm in, where being this man's captive is a better fate than being set free because of my financial situation. In the back of my mind these weeks, I've feared he would eventually kill me, but it never ever occurred to me that I should worry about going back to the problems I was in before captivity.

He's still stroking my hair, his fingertips moving down to rub the back of my neck. I'm ashamed of how much I love it when he does this. It still feels so wrong to love anything that comes from his hand, especially since I have guilt-free pleasure with Seven. Both men are equally beautiful, but one is a monster, and I can't let myself feel anything for him, so I push these things down as much as I can.

"Don't worry, Kate, I won't let you starve. I'm prepared to offer you two million dollars."

My breath stops for a second, and maybe my heart as well. I can't have heard him right. Is he paying me for my silence? Or is this just another sick game? What's the catch?

"Unfortunately, this offer is only for you. If you accept, I'll have to kill your companion. But you'll be free and safe. I think it's a pretty good offer. You should carefully consider your answer."

I'm stunned for a moment. Why would he let me go but not Seven?

"No!" I say as soon as I can get my vocal cords to work again. My refusal comes out shrill and panicked.

He shrugs. "I could just kill you both. I'm offended that you would spit on my generosity in this way."

I'm crying now, great heaving sobs that I can't get

control of. "Please, please..." I whimper.

Then I hear Seven's quiet, strong voice rising above my crying and begging. "Take the deal, Kitten," he says.

I extricate myself from the hand still stroking the nape of my neck. Our captor acts as if this entire conversation were about something unimportant—not two lives hanging in the balance. But our lives *are* unimportant to him. I crawl the few feet to Seven and bury my face in his chest. I'm grateful the chains give enough leeway for him to put his arms around me. He strokes my back.

"Shhhh," he says. "I'll be fine. Don't worry about me. I need you to go. Live your life."

I shake my head, my tears dripping onto his chest. "No, I won't leave you. I love you."

I involuntarily flinch when I say this because I remember our captor is standing so close. He heard this confession of love, and he surely won't be happy about it.

There's a long beat of tense silence, and then Seven laughs. It's a dark, sinister laugh, like nothing I've heard from him before.

"What was that, Declan? Three weeks?" Seven says. "Impressive. I thought she'd take the money."

I pull away from Seven to look in his eyes, still not believing what I've just heard. This can't be real. I trusted him. I thought that he... I thought he was like me...

"You are *so* adorable," Seven says. "So sweetly trusting. I love it."

"No! No, no no..." I can't stop the word. It's gotten stuck on repeat. I scramble back to the corner I was in only minutes ago when Declan first stepped into the room.

I'm still trying to put it all together. I had thought Seven was my captor that first day, but I'd become quickly convinced by the lie of his innocence which only became more convincing the more time passed. And after the way he was tossed in the cell all bloody and broken the day we were punished for speaking each other's names in the seemingly safe space of the shower... Did he *let* Declan beat him like that?

It's strange having a name for my captor now... my *other* captor. Declan unchains Seven, and the two of them stand together, watching me, amusement on their triumphant faces. It was a game, and Seven won. Good for him.

I seek desperately to put together a new narrative of what really happened these past weeks. Obviously, he did let Declan beat him that day, something I can't begin to comprehend. But it served its purpose. It convinced me we were *in this together*. That we were a team. Us against the monster. It bonded me to him more tightly than any other play they could have made.

Did they plan and coordinate each move? Did Seven know ahead of time how every last detail would unfold? When Declan was keeping me in his bedroom and blind-folding me to take me to the dungeon... Seven had to have been walking around free outside the cell. Did he watch? Did he become the new voyeur?

I squeeze my eyes shut, trying not to think about the fact that while I worried Declan was starving him and beating him, or had even killed him, that he was just taking a break from the *game*.

Whenever Seven was dragged out of the cell, Declan wasn't moving him long distances to punish him or whatever. It was all just a show until he got out into the hallway.

Seven knew there were no real drugs in the syringe the day of the escape attempt. He knew Declan was lying there fully conscious waiting for us to almost get free before pulling the rug out.

Another realization slams into me like a mallet. Seven was never drugged. The food he ate was the same as mine. And every time he was injected with what I thought were drugs, it was only a saline solution. Nothing was real.

Declan told the truth every time he said Seven wasn't my hero and everything was an act and a game. He put the truth right under my nose in plain sight. He openly stated it while I thought he was just taunting me.

"You're going to kill me aren't you?" I say, the tears still flowing down my cheeks. I *loved* Seven. God help me, but I still love him.

"No," Seven says. "We really are letting you go. I mean there's only so long I can live in a cell with nothing else to do. So here's the deal. You will sign a non-disclosure agreement, backdated to the date that we took you. The contract states that you were here of your own free will playing a game with us. You can tell no one about anything that has happened here."

I wish it was Declan telling me all this because it's so hard to see this change in Seven. I thought he cared about me... I thought...

"You will not go to the police. We own nearly every judge in this corrupt city, and we can guarantee we would get one of those judges should a trial ever occur. And we own about half the police. If you go to one of our guys, he'll just bring you right back to us, and we will be very displeased. You can't imagine the punishment."

"Master, please..." I can't dwell on this betrayal because starvation is still a real possibility, and I have nowhere to go, and I'm sure the money was part of their sick joke—the carrot they could take away as soon as my greedy little eyes lit upon it. "Please... I have nowhere to go," I say quietly.

"Yes, you do," Seven says. "Declan has set up a bank account in your name, and we have all the paperwork and bank cards for you. The account has five million dollars in it. You also now own a penthouse apartment in the city, fully furnished. And a car, a blue Porsche 911 Carrera. You're welcome."

I shake my head. "It's not real. You're just fucking with me again." I can't take any more of these lies.

Seven steps out of the cell for a moment, the keypad accepting his thumbprint as easily as Declan's. As if I needed any more proof of his role in this. No wonder Declan made me call Seven, *master*.

I cry harder now as I'm left alone in the room with Declan. The bad master. The scary one. But they are both utterly terrifying now. They were just playing good cop/bad cop with me, and I was too stupid to see it.

"You're both psychopaths," I whisper.

"Oh, come now, Pretty Toy. If we were psychopaths, you'd be dead right now. We're sociopaths."

"What's the difference?" I never actually thought there was a difference. I've heard the terms used interchangeably so many times.

Declan walks over to me. I cringe away from him, my back now pressed against the wall with no more room to run. He sits on the ground beside me, stroking my hair.

"Sociopaths can form bonds with a select few people. And lucky for you, you're now one of those people."

I don't believe him. I can't. The amount of deceit both men have used with me these past few weeks is too great for me to believe a word out of their pathologically lying mouths.

"Did I ever once threaten your life?" he asks.

"No." He did mention starving, but I know he means violent immediate murder threats. It's fucked-up that I can read between his lines and know what he means even if he isn't entirely specific.

"No, *what*? You aren't free quite yet. Let's not get too casual."

"N-no, Master." I can't stop crying.

"Good girl. Did either of us ever physically harm you in any serious way? Any broken bones? Cutting? Amputations? Starvation? And I mean actual starvation, refusing you food with no way for you to rectify that situation. Were you at any point violently raped?"

"No, Master," I whisper.

"That's what I thought." He stands back up as Seven re-enters the room with some papers, a pen, and the clothes I was wearing the night I was taken. The little black dress. He takes me by the arm and guides me to the bathroom where the light is better. The latest white roses are wilting in the vase. Some of the petals have fallen onto the counter.

It's jarring, because there were always fresh roses. They never got to this state before being replaced with more, always while I was sleeping.

"Read, sign, and initial in the marked places," he says.

Seven strokes my back as I read. I hate him more than Declan right now. At least I always knew Declan was the bad guy. Seven's betrayal cuts deeper.

I can barely read through my tears but I get the gist of it. It doesn't even matter what the fuck these papers say. I have no choice but to sign them. I'm not really agreeing to anything, just obeying one more of their whims.

I sign and initial in all the appropriate places.

"Good girl," Seven says, passing the papers to Declan. "Now get dressed, and I'll take you to your new home."

My hands shake as I put on the bra, panties, dress, and heels. It feels so uncomfortably strange to have fabric resting against my skin after so much time naked.

He pulls a black scrap of fabric out of his pocket and ties it around my eyes.

When I panic, he says, "It's just until we get away from the house."

He leads me out of the cell, down a hallway, out a front door. Birds are chirping as he opens a car door and guides me inside.

"Buckle up," he says before shutting me into the silence of the car.

He joins me a moment later and the engine revs to life. As we drive, I wonder how many women they've done this to.

There's this sick part of me that still wants to be with Seven because a part of my mind is still in shock and can't accept that he's the bad guy. I'm still not sure he's not just taking me somewhere to kill me. His level of elaborate deceit makes anything now possible.

But I don't ask or beg because if he were planning to

kill me, he wouldn't tell me the truth about it anyway. I remember what Declan said back in the cell about how sociopaths could form a few limited bonds. Maybe they know they have to kill me but don't want me to see it coming. Maybe this is their twisted way of showing mercy.

With a blindfold, I wouldn't see it coming. Seven could just park the car somewhere, reach over and snap my neck. If he kills me, I hope he does it like that. Quick, where I don't see it coming.

"I can't believe I believed you. I believed you cared..." I say, needing to talk to get my mind off the dark fears consuming me.

"Shhh," he says before I can start sobbing again. His hand strokes my knee, and I can't bring myself to pull away, and it isn't the fear. I hate myself right now for still wanting him to touch me.

"Don't feel bad," he says. "There are women married for decades to serial killers, with children even. They never suspect. Without a real conscience, it's easy to hide, and normal people can't even fathom what goes on inside our minds. And you never really know anyone anyway. Everything you think you know about anyone you've ever met is just the parts they've shown you. You never really know anyone," he says again. Does he really believe this? I'm not sure. Maybe it's true though.

We always have a skewed perspective of other people, even those closest to us. We make shorthand assumptions about their thoughts and feelings and motivations. We project ourselves onto them. We become disillusioned when we find out we were wrong about people.

My hands are clenched together in my lap. "I felt safe with you."

"You were safe with me. You're still safe with me. Tell me, Kitten, if you needed surgery, would you prefer to have someone very empathetic or very sociopathic operate on you?"

What kind of question is this? "Someone empathetic, of course."

He laughs. "No, you wouldn't. Very empathetic people are the type of people who break down into tears when a disaster happens on the other side of the world to random strangers they've never met. They hold candlelight vigils and pray and wring their hands. They see a starving African child on a television commercial and send money they probably could put to better use for their own family because they felt sad seeing a small sad-eyed hungry child. And they need to assuage their guilt at having a full belly. They are altruistic even to the point of neglecting their own needs or their family's needs. They have no strong loyalties because they love everyone with a shallow love that is really just their lack of emotional control."

I let these words fall over me. I don't know if I should believe them, but they do sound true. I've known people like this. Every news story depresses them or makes them anxious. They get emotionally over-involved in the lives of strangers.

"It's not black or white, Kate. I guarantee you every top surgeon in the world is at least a bit sociopathic. You have to be able to shut your feelings off and just see a body in front of you so you can make clear-headed rational choices. You don't want someone who is too emotional or falls apart at every little thing or feels everybody else's emotions. Most politicians are sociopaths. Most CEOs are sociopaths. And yet the world still spins."

"You didn't really feel anything for me. I didn't expect Declan to, but I thought you..."

"Obviously, I felt something, Kitten. He does, too."

And that's all I'm going to get from him. I know this because he seems to become a wall. He turns on the radio to a classical music station, and we drive the rest of the way in silence.

Finally the car stops, he removes the blindfold from my eyes, and he gives me a folder with all my bank stuff, my purse, and a set of keys.

"Your car is in the parking garage. And you live on the top floor." He winks at me. "It's where they typically keep the penthouse. Goodbye, Kate."

I swallow back the tears. I'm never going to see this man again. I shouldn't want to see him again. And now that I know they were both bad, it seems stupid to deny I also felt something for Declan. Because one of them isn't the safe guilt-free choice anymore. They were both evil. And suddenly, in this moment, I'm flooded with my feelings for Declan, these soft feelings I've denied myself because it was so wrong.

I get out of the car, and before I close the door, I say, "Can I ask you one more question?"

"Ask," he says.

"How do you know Declan?"

"My only friend since childhood. He was the one person I knew who was like me. Empty."

These are the last words he says to me. I shut the car

door and watch him drive away. I manage to get inside the building and onto the elevator, riding up to the penthouse before I break down into sobs again. I feel so lonely and so wrong in every way one can be wrong.

I feel... discarded. And I am. But at least I won't starve.

I'm surprised when the elevator doors open directly into the penthouse. I had to use a key in the elevator for this floor, but I still somehow expected a hallway. There are floor-to-ceiling windows, and the view is astounding.

I drop my purse, keys, and large bank envelope onto a chair next to the elevator. And then I freeze. Right in front of me, on a marble table, is a vase of fresh fragrant white roses. There's a card in the flowers with my name on it.

My hand shakes as I pull out the card.

When you are ready to come home, call, and we will come get you.

There's a phone number at the bottom.

They're still playing with me. They think I'm so addicted to what they turned me into that I will give up freedom and luxury to go back to them and live in a cell like some animal.

Fuck them both.

I pick up the vase of flowers and hurl it against the wall. The glass shatters into hundreds of tiny shards. I rip up the card with the number on it and throw it in the trash. I will not play their new game.

9

An entire week passes before I finally clean up the shattered glass, water, and now wilted roses. I feel inexplicably sad that the life has gone out of them. It's another week before I start to regret throwing the card away. It's long gone now and in a landfill.

During the first few days of my freedom I went to the spa and got every treatment on the menu in a full-day pampering frenzy. It was nice, but massages and body masks and wraps and a mani-pedi cannot erase the memory of their hands on my body, their dark voices in my ear.

I've also shopped. I bought a whole new wardrobe. Nice things. I went out to nice restaurants and contemplated how to get myself out of the self-imposed isolation I'd created, how to form some real and lasting social bonds. I need some friends, but I'm not sure how to do that. Maybe I could volunteer somewhere?

I sit on the floor next to the window in the main open

floor plan living area, thinking about my options. Part of me wants to open my own ad agency. I've got the resources now, and I could probably get a few of my old clients to come to me. I could even work here from my new home. There's plenty of room to set up a business and meet clients. But I need time to wallow and ... mourn them.

I feel so wrong and twisted for mourning, but I have so many memories of Seven being so kind. Comforting me. Being gentle. The ugly truth can't erase all the beautiful moments we shared, even if they were never real.

Declan was kind in his own way. He never used violence to break me. He used fear and kindness. Pleasure.

Even if I still had their number, I wouldn't call. There's no way I would ever voluntarily place myself in their hands again no matter how much it haunts my dreams, no matter how many times I bring myself to orgasm when I wake up to find they aren't there. These men are evil. They are dangerous. And it doesn't matter if they told me they felt some *bond* with me or that I'm somehow safe. I know I'm not.

And yet, I also know they know exactly where I am. They could come take me back at any time. So why haven't I used this money to flee the country? Why haven't I transferred the money to another bank, something they don't have access to, because they no doubt have access to the account they set up for me. Why don't I ditch the car and get a new one? Sell the penthouse and pocket the cash? Because I'm stupid and pathetic and some sick part of me hopes they'll come take me so that it's not my fault when this inevitably ends in my grisly death. They are still toying with me, still playing a game. I know this, but I make no move to take my game piece off the board.

My piece is still in play. I know it, and I'm sure they know it.

My eyes light on my handbag, the one that went with the little black dress. It's still sitting on the chair beside the elevator. I actually burned that dress and the panties and bra I was wearing, but I haven't touched the bag. It's partly because it's a sleek, sophisticated black Louis Vuitton that I bought as a splurge when I got my first major promotion at the agency. It has sentimental value even as it also has these conflicted memories now attached.

I can't burn it or throw it out, so it just sat there. My phone is also in there. It's kind of amazing how you can get away without having a cell phone in a big city when you don't really have anyone to call anyway. The penthouse has a landline, so it isn't as though I'm totally without communication to the outside world. And I have a laptop now and the internet. I kind of really missed the internet during those weeks of unreality, playing their game.

I've been trying to think of it that way, that I somehow chose to play. I've been trying to convince myself that the contract I signed is somehow the real story of what went down. Just some kinky games and fun. Just a fantasy that went for a few weeks and now it's over. I've been compensated handsomely for my participation. And now I can move on into a wonderful new life. But can I really?

I pick myself up off the ground and cross to the chair and my bag. I open the sleek black handbag to find my wallet with a small bit of cash untouched and my credit cards. I should probably pay them off now that I can afford to. There's also a nude lipstick, a mirror, and my phone.

I pull out the phone. I don't know why I expected after a month to be able to just turn it on. Of course the battery is dead. I sigh. I need to get out anyway.

I go by the closest cell phone store. I was on auto-pay, and I'm comforted to find out that the most recent payment charge went through. I get a new charger and stop by a small corner Chinese buffet for some lo mein, sweet and sour chicken, and egg rolls.

Even with money, the issues in my life haven't gone away. I didn't realize how lonely I was. And maybe that's why I think of them so much, why I still crave them so much. I return home and charge the phone, determined that I'm going to find a way to reconnect with people.

While the numbers in my contact list weren't close enough to go to when destitute, I can certainly get together with someone for drinks, especially if I'm buying. It's a start.

When the phone is charged, I'm unsurprised to find I have messages and voice mails. All from Andrew. There are about ten text messages and fifteen voicemails.

The texts are basically: "Where are you?" "I can't find you." "Did you give me the right address?" "Did you mean this restaurant or that one on the corner of Fifth and Main with a similar name?" "Are you fucking with me?" "Why won't you text me back?" "Hello?" "Hello?" "Bitch."

The voice mails are far more abusive. The words "lying whore" and "worthless piece of trash" are colorfully interspersed with "fuck you" and "bitch".

As I listen to this unrelenting stream of man-child

screaming, it occurs to me that my captors never screamed at me or called me names. I mean, yes, Declan called me a whore, but it didn't feel like this. Somehow, even though I knew he was the bad guy, it felt almost like an endearment from his lips.

I delete all the messages and texts and block Andrew's number. I don't see a reason to respond to him or ever contact him again. I scroll through the contact list to find someone for those theoretical "on me" drinks, when I find there's a new contact that I didn't put in there. The names Seven and Declan are listed as a single contact in my list.

I want to push the delete button, but I can't bring myself to do it. The strongest feeling I have when I see their number is relief. I have access. It's as though the card from the flowers reassembled and flew back to me from the trash. This time I have to keep it safe.

But I won't call. I will not call them. It's just nice to know I can.

That's the most disturbing thought I've had in a long time. It's nice to know I can? What the fuck have they done to me?

I try to make myself delete it again, but this time, insanely, I press the call button. It rings twice, and I end the call before anyone answers. I spend five minutes staring at the screen, waiting for it to light up and ring, for them to call me back. But they don't.

Maybe they're doing this with someone else now. I waited too long, and now they're playing the game with somebody new. I shudder at that thought and the actual bit of jealousy it inspires. I should feel sorry for the poor girl, whoever she is, horrified by her situation, not jealous that it isn't me.

I call a girl named Julie from my contacts. When she answers, she says she wondered what happened with me, and she hated to see me leave the agency. Says it was nice to have a little less testosterone there. We agree to meet for drinks on Friday.

10

Friday night and three drinks too many sees me flopping face down onto a gray leather sofa in the penthouse at two in the morning. I get a text. Julie making sure I got home okay. I let her know I did, make sure she did, too, then flop back against the leather.

She's nice enough, but there isn't really a strong friend connection there. I scroll through the contact list, landing once again on Seven and Declan. Alcohol and cell phones are really bad combinations for me. I know this. It's how that sad clown phone call to Andrew happened.

I'm not calling them. Yes, let's call two psychos who spent three weeks fucking me in every way one can be fucked both physically and mentally, in the middle of the night. What could possibly go wrong?

But drunk Kate is not strong enough to stop herself from pushing the call button.

Seven answers on the third ring. "Hello, Kate."

I have visions of Hannibal Lector at this smooth

greeting at two o'clock in the morning. Suddenly I feel stone-cold sober. I bolt upright on the sofa, gripping the phone like a lifeline. I should hang up, but I don't. I just want to hear his voice.

"Hey, Seven," I say, trying to sound casual as though we once had a few nice dates and I'm just calling to catch up.

"I'm sorry, that's not my name, and you know it."

"Master," I correct. I can't help that this word goes straight to my pussy. They've trained me so well. And they knew I would call and beg to come back to my cage. Though I haven't sunk quite so low yet.

"Better," he says. "Now what can I do for you?" His voice is so calm and in control, and I crave everything that voice is right now. I crave their calm control even as I know how messed up it is.

"I'm sorry, I shouldn't have called. It's late. I had some drinks. I'm... I'm sorry."

His voice is low and soft when he speaks again. "Do you want us to come get you and bring you back home, Kitten?"

I try to keep my tears quiet, but I'm sure he can hear them. "Yes, Master," I whisper. And it's true.

I'm in so much trouble.

THE WORDS *SEVEN AND DECLAN* LIGHT UP MY PHONE SCREEN when it rings.

"Master?" I say when I answer.

"Good girl," Seven says. "I'm here. Come to the parking

garage. Bring nothing but your keys." He disconnects the call before I can respond.

Suddenly I'm nothing but doubt and anxiety. What am I doing? Why would I hand myself back over to them? Yet even as I silently ask the question, I know why. At the sound of his voice in my ear, with only those few words, my body is alive, awake in a way it hasn't been awake since they released me.

I shove the keys into the pocket of my jeans.

When I enter the parking garage, he's leaning against an understated gold Maserati, his arms crossed casually over his chest, his gaze locked on mine. Some fucked-up broken part of me wants to kneel at his feet and wait for the praise as he pets my hair and calls me his good girl, but I resist. This is a public place, and even in the middle of the night, anyone could stumble upon us.

I want to run back inside and lock myself inside the penthouse. The fact that he has this effect on me even after everything has me scared of him in an entirely new way.

"I missed you, Kitten."

He pushes off the car then unlocks and opens the passenger side for me. I get in and jump when the door shuts. Before I can do something sane, like open my door and run, he's in the driver's seat, the car is starting, and we're moving.

The drive back *home* is silent except for the sound of classical music coming in through the sound system. I wonder if Seven is the classical music lover or if both of them are. The drive is longer than I remember, and it becomes obvious the longer we drive that it truly is out in the middle of nowhere.

We're driving now on an old road without any street lights, with endless old and thick gnarled trees lined up, their branches and leaves canopying over us, inviting us ominously into the deep, dark wood. I feel like red riding hood, and my driver is the wolf.

After what feels like an endless drive in this densely wooded area, we finally come upon a huge iron gate. He presses a button on a remote control, and it slides open without complaint. Now there are lights every few yards, and the landscape is what I remember, the endless gently rolling hills free of trees. I look back to see a high wall winding around the perimeter of the property.

Now *this* road feels like it goes on forever. The anticipation is killing me. Finally we reach... well, house isn't exactly the word I'd use. Since I wasn't allowed to roam freely, I never knew just how big it was. But house is far too mild a description. Estate? Mansion? Palace? Resort? Nothing really seems expansive enough to explain where they live.

It looks a bit like a fairy tale castle. Huge, imposing, and regal. But it's not the kind of fairy tale most of us dream about. There are all sorts of spotlights around the place, aimed up, illuminating it in the darkness, making it seem even more impressive than it might be in the day. There is an enormous fountain in the front with similar lighting, making already spooky gargoyles look all the more imposing. In any other circumstance, I might think the gargoyles were over-the-top, but there are several guarding the rooftops as well, and honestly? It works in a villain fortress sort of way.

"I forgot you haven't actually seen the house from the

outside," Seven says. Apparently he thinks the word *house* is just fine. "What do you think? Better than your penthouse?" he says with gentle teasing. It's that charming facade that falls so easily into place with him that it lets me forget for a moment what lies beneath.

He pulls the car into a circular driveway, then he takes me in the front door as though I'm a normal guest coming here for a normal reason. I don't know why, but for some reason, I thought he'd sneak me in through a back servant entrance as though there were people to hide me from. I know for sure there's a cleaning service, even though I've yet to encounter them directly.

Declan is waiting on a sofa against the wall when we walk in.

He winks at me when I catch that gray gaze which seems the smallest degree warmer than I've ever seen it. Maybe I'm seeing what I want to see—something to convince me that this isn't crazy, putting myself back in the hands of these two psychos.

"Welcome home, Pretty Toy."

My stomach does a little flip at this, and a longing I'd almost made myself forget comes rushing back to the surface, igniting the place between my legs with warm liquid heat.

"I'm going to get her settled," Seven says. "Come, Kitten."

I tear my gaze from Declan and follow Seven wordlessly up a grand staircase and down a long wide hallway. "This is your room," he says, stopping in front of a large room halfway down the hall.

Gauzy transparent white curtains hang in front of the

windows, and even from the doorway, I can see there are French doors that go out onto a balcony. It's a beautiful room. Blond hardwood floors, a king-sized canopy bed with that same gauzy fabric. With a canopy bed, it should look like a little girl's room, but it's the grown-up sophisticated version. The furniture is all natural light-colored wood, with a few gold accents like the full-length leaner mirror on one side wall. Somehow it doesn't look gauche. The walls are a pale cream.

On a table beside the balcony doors is a large vase of fragrant white roses. The room has an attached bathroom, but I can't see inside it from my vantage point.

"What? But I thought..." I stop myself before the sentence is out fully in the open air for us all to stare at it and ponder how idiotic it is.

"You thought you were going back to the cell?"

I look down, unable to meet his eyes suddenly. "Yes."

"Do you *want* to go back to the cell?"

"N-no, Master, I just thought..." Again I stop because I shouldn't question it. If I don't have to sleep on a bare mattress—however nice—in a dark gray cell, I should not call attention to the fact that that's an actual option.

"Once the puppy is trained, it doesn't have to stay in the crate. And you are definitely trained," Seven says.

Declan only chuckles at this. He must have followed us up the stairs. I was too busy being in awe of my gilded cage to notice.

Being back with them, it's becoming increasingly obvious that Seven is the real game maker. He's the one running everything, pulling all the strings behind the scenes. Declan is just as responsible, of course. He was a happy and willing participant, but this is Seven's game. It always has been.

I was always wrong about who had the power here. It's so much more obvious now that Seven isn't playing his role as my co-captive. He stands taller and broader than his friend and partner in crime. I know Declan can hold his own, but there's a subtle deference he shows Seven. I didn't notice it the day I learned the truth, but it's so clear now.

Not only is Seven the one in charge, but I'm now sure he's the most dangerous of the two—and I slept trustingly inside the circle of his arms on that mattress for weeks while he stroked my hair, got me off, and whispered soothing words into my ear.

The tears come out of nowhere. Maybe not out of nowhere, but I'm sure that's how it appears to these men who have trained me to think of them as my masters.

"Kate?" Seven says. He looks concerned that I'm crying. He wears the mask so well, and it hurts even more when he plays this game with me. At least I always got the truth with Declan. That cold emptiness. But Seven still likes to pretend he has something inside.

And I still want so badly to believe it.

He steps closer to me, and I instinctively take a step back. He arches a brow. I called *him* after all. Nobody forced me to come back here, but it's hard not to take a step back. He seems so much taller now that he's not my protector.

He takes another step closer, and I fight the urge to run. A long shuddering breath flows out of me as he looks down at me and strokes the side of my cheek. I lean into him, my eyes drifting closed before I can stop them. He pulls me into his arms and strokes my hair.

"Shhhh," he murmurs as though he actually cares. And I want to believe. I find myself leaning more heavily against him as a wave of dizziness washes over me. I'd sobered up pretty quickly after calling them—or I thought I did. But I did have a lot of alcohol. And I know it was just the adrenaline overriding everything else going on in my body, making me think I was okay when I'm not.

"Declan," he says quietly, "she needs to eat. Will you bring something up?"

I don't hear an answer, only the receding of footsteps out of the room.

Seven undresses me and puts me in the bed, then he sits on the edge, watching me for several minutes. Finally he sighs and says, "It's late. After you eat, I want you to sleep. We'll discuss what comes next in the morning."

I can't help tensing at these words. But he only takes my hand in his, stroking the back of it, still soothing me.

Declan comes up a little while later with some food. It's a chicken salad sandwich on toasted bread with a huge tomato on it. And some baked barbeque potato chips. He leaves the plate of food and a glass of water on the bedside table.

"Thank you," I say.

Now it's his turn to arch a brow.

"M-master," I add quickly.

He nods.

It's not that I forgot; I just wasn't sure how things were supposed to be now. What are the new rules? With Seven in charge, I just don't know. Seven turns on the bedside lamp, then both men leave the room, turning off the main light and shutting the door behind them. The lock is on the inside, so they can't lock me in. It's a small relief.

If I weren't still so drunk, I might be tempted to sneak out and explore the house, but I feel awful, and I'm so tired. I somehow manage to eat the food without getting sick. I really did need it. It was too much alcohol swirling around without any kind of buffer. I'm about to turn off the lamp when I spot a card sticking out of the roses. I struggle to stand and move toward the card as though in a trance. With shaking hands, I slide the card out of its small envelope.

Welcome home, Kitten. There's no going back now.

The piece of stiff ecru paper falls from my hand onto the hardwood floor. I don't bother to pick it up. I'm afraid bending over would just make me feel dizzy again. I open the balcony door and step outside for some fresh air, trying to settle my now pounding heart as I worry about the sinister promises in those words.

The view from here is different from the ones I've glimpsed through hallway and kitchen windows on the first floor. This view overlooks an enormous garden of white roses, illuminated by an intricate patchwork of outdoor lighting. So not only do they have a cleaning service, they have landscapers and gardeners.

The scent wafts to my nose on the breeze. It's sweet and fragrant but not cloying. It makes me feel calm even when I know I shouldn't. I look down over the ornate iron railing. It's a high drop, and I know there's a big wall around the perimeter anyway. I wish I hadn't had so many drinks tonight. Drunk Kate is Stupid Kate. And the extreme truth

of that is only just now beginning to sink into my aware-
ness past the fog of an unfortunate number of tequila
shots.

I stumble back into the bedroom, turn off the lamp,
and slide between the cool silk sheets. The world shuts off
as soon as my head touches the pillow.

11

I wake in pitch blackness. Even with windows in this room, it's so dark I may as well be blindfolded. I don't know if the moon is dark tonight or if clouds are covering it, but being out as far as we are, there are no street lights. And they've obviously shut off the outdoor lighting.

It only takes a moment to realize why I've woken. I feel him beside me in the bed. I don't mean physically—skin against skin. I just know I'm not alone. And I know it's Seven. I realize suddenly how I know. It's his scent. The clean, safe maleness of him. I've associated his scent with safety for so long, my brain can't rewrite the code now.

I let out a surprised gasp when he pulls back the blankets, exposing my body to the cool air of the room. I wonder if he can see me, if he's using whatever night vision assistance Declan used when he would come into the cell at night, switching out Seven's clothes and the roses on the bathroom counter.

My legs fall open without his command, and he begins to stroke me just like he used to do inside the cell. It doesn't take long for my moans and whimpers to fill the darkness and then only a short while longer for me to come.

"Sleep, Kitten," he whispers. He covers me back up, and I feel his weight lift off the bed. The door opens, letting the smallest whisper of distant light drift in, then I'm alone again, still panting.

I've got a headache when I wake to the sunlight streaming in through the windows and balcony door a few hours later. Seven is already beside me with some aspirin and water. Then he's feeding me again in bed—a big plate of soft scrambled eggs and dry toast.

"How do you feel, Kitten?" he asks after I've eaten.

"Bad."

And I must look it, too, because he doesn't get angry about the lack of title or punish me. He just takes the plate and glass away. He pulls the blinds and curtains on the window and balcony door, giving me as much darkness as the day will allow and leaves.

He returns a few minutes later and puts another glass of water on the bedside table then presses a kiss to my forehead before shutting the door and leaving me alone to sleep it off.

I lie in bed for a while, unable to fall back asleep, trying to figure out what his angle is. He seems so much like the Seven I thought I knew from the cell that it makes my heart hurt. It's so cruel that he would play with me like this —give me this lie when what's really inside him is cold, swirling darkness threatening to capsize my mind at any moment.

Why the fuck did I call? The words on the card repeat over and over in my mind. *No going back now.* I roll over, pull the blankets over my head, and drift back to sleep.

IT'S JUST PAST THREE IN THE AFTERNOON WHEN I WAKE. There's a clock on the wall just across from me. I feel a thousand times better than I did this morning, but I feel gross. I use the bathroom and take a shower, feeling more human with each step into this routine of normalcy which distracts me from what could be coming as soon as I'm well enough.

The bathroom matches the bedroom more or less. It's weirdly not quite as nice as the one attached to the cell, but there's a shower and a claw foot bathtub next to a large picture window, so it's nice enough. Even if we weren't so isolated, being on the second floor, no one could see in, but I can still see the rose garden, at least when I stand looking directly outside.

I return to the bedroom with a towel wrapped around me, startled to find both Seven and Declan standing in the room waiting, arms crossed over chests as though they are my bodyguards rather than my captors. *Captors I ran back to,* I remind myself. With every minute of full sobriety, I realize my foolishness, how I've sealed my fate.

"Feeling better, Kitten?"

"Y-yes, Master."

"Good, now drop the towel and kneel."

The air goes out of my lungs, and both the fear and excitement I haven't felt in weeks is back in one sudden rush. And yet I feel self-conscious. I had gotten so used to being their naked caged animal, but now I've become used to the civilizing influence of clothing. I unconsciously clutch the fabric tight across myself.

"I don't want to start with punishment," Seven says.

I take a deep breath and let the towel fall. Then I kneel on a soft pale rug in front of them.

"Good girl." This time it's Declan who speaks.

Seven reaches behind him to pick up something from the bed. It's a round silver-colored metal band. There are glittering pale pink gemstones inlaid in the metal, which is probably platinum. He uses a key to unlock it, then puts it around my throat and locks it in place.

"The collar doesn't come off. It's safe to get it wet. Every day you'll be allowed to leave the property from eleven in the morning until six in the evening. The penthouse, car, and money remain yours."

They're letting me come and go? How do they know I won't run if whatever this is becomes too much for me? It's possible this question is plainly readable on my face because Seven's next words are: "There's a tracking device in the collar. Don't make us chase you."

So not really free, just a very long leash. I'm still confused by their generosity. I can't square it with what they've done to me. And I can't figure out where exactly they exist on the good and evil scale. I keep foolishly wanting to believe maybe they aren't that evil. But even I can't pretend they've only engaged in a little harmless coloring outside the moral lines.

"Let's take her to the dungeon," Declan says. "We have more interesting things down there."

"True, and we can finally play without the pretense."

A strangled sob escapes my throat at this pronouncement.

"Shhh, Pretty Toy. We don't hurt good girls, and you're going to be our good girl, right?"

"Y-yes, Master."

I'm already mentally plotting ways to escape. I can use my "prison yard time" to find someone who can get this fucking collar off me and transfer money out of that account and get the fuck as far from them as possible—like I should have done from the beginning. It doesn't matter how much I want and need them to touch me. I cannot continue down this road.

Declan chuckles, as though he can read these thoughts right out of my head. And probably he can. I'm not able to hide my true feelings in the way they can behind a face trained to show the expected emotions.

"You will not seek help from any of the staff as they come and go. They're all here illegally. They know the consequences of interfering in our personal affairs. And you will be seriously punished," Declan says.

I swallow hard and nod my understanding. I believe him. Somehow I know I've never been seriously punished by them. I may have been played with and by them, but my punishments have been warnings... tastes of theoretical terrors should I breach the limits of their patience.

Seven helps me to stand, and they lead me downstairs,

back down that long hallway to the dungeon. My heart is beating so fast, and I don't know if it's fear or arousal.

The dungeon feels different now. As much as I loved the Seven who I thought was trying to protect me, I also kind of hated him. I hated that extra bit of shame I felt because he wasn't fully on board. I hated that I had to carry that shame long after I was already broken and ready to please and be pleased by both of them.

He was always the holdout, except that he never was.

When we get to the dungeon, I kneel again. I don't wait to be commanded. I just do it.

"Good girl," Seven says. It continues to feel strange when he takes this role that had previously only been Declan's domain. He bends down, his hand going between my legs. "I think it's time to wax this pussy, don't you, Kitten?"

My breath goes shallow. "Y-yes, Master."

"I'll heat the wax," Declan says, disappearing into the adjacent bathroom.

I'm scared now because waxing hurts, and I don't have the greatest pain threshold. After a while, you get used to it, and it's not so bad when a professional does it. But Seven and Declan aren't professionals, and I'm afraid it will hurt more because of that. But I don't voice this concern. I do, however, wish that I'd made a waxing appointment for Friday before I went out for drinks. I knew it was about time to do it, but I was so wrapped up in my own self-pity —poor little newly rich girl—that it didn't occur to me.

Seven helps me off the floor and guides me to a St. Andrew's Cross leaned against one exposed brick wall. I've never been bound to this before. Spanking benches, yes.

And the bondage bed was Declan's favorite. It's convenient and far more comfortable than it looks.

"M-Master? Did I do something wrong?"

He laughs at this. "I haven't gotten to punish you yet. Don't you think I should get to?"

"Yes, Master." It's almost a whisper.

"I could give you a list of your minor missteps, all adding up to a justification, but I don't need a justification. You are *mine*. I will do whatever I want with you."

Suddenly, the waxing is the last thing on my mind.

He nods toward the St. Andrew's Cross. I turn away from him and spread my arms and legs out so he can bind me to the end points. I close my eyes. I don't want to watch him picking whatever it is he plans to use on me. I hope it's not the cane.

I cry out at the unexpected pain of a paddle landing hard against my ass. In its own way it's just as bad as the cane. The tears come immediately after only the first blow. He rubs my heated flesh.

"Yes, Kitten. I like how you don't hold back. Let me have those pretty tears. I'm jealous you only gave them to Declan for so long."

He paddles me as though I truly have done something worthy of punishment, and something about this particular implement makes me feel contrite even as the space between my legs responds with arousal.

He stops and presses his body against mine. I feel his erection through his pants. He steps away again and gives me another hard smack with the paddle. I'm blubbering and sobbing.

"Please," I whimper. If I knew of some wrong I'd

committed that deserved punishment I would beg forgiveness, but I know he's doing this for his own gratification.
He strokes my skin again and presses a kiss to my tear-
streaked cheek.

"Shhhh, Kitten."

Then there is a vibrating toy between my legs. I squirm
and twist trying to gain more contact every time he pulls it
away. Unlike Declan, he likes to tease me with the lowest
setting so long that I think I'll lose my mind from it.

"Master, please..."

I want the toy inside me. For some reason in the time I
was apart from them, when I masturbated, I stayed on the
outside. I couldn't bring myself to change the way I
touched myself alone. I couldn't admit they'd changed me
and what my body craves forever. Now I *need* to come that
way. I need Seven to shove the toy inside me. Or his fingers.
Or his cock. Anything. But he only presses the vibrator
harder against my clit until I come, bucking against it and
his hand.

"The wax is on the warmer. It's ready when you are,"
Declan says.

"In a minute. I'm not done here yet. We need to retrain
her ass. It's been weeks. Unless she was putting things
inside her own ass in our absence," he says, amusement
threading his voice. "*Were* you doing that, Kitten?"

"N-no, Master."

He sighs. "Such a shame. I would have jerked off to that
thought for ages."

I take a slow, deep breath when he slides a toy heavy
with lube into my ass. It feels far better than it should after
such a long break. I find myself moving with it, thrusting

my ass back toward him trying to get deeper penetration with the toy.

"I told you she was becoming an anal slut," Declan says.

I flush hot at these words, but I can't stop myself from seeking more contact with the toy he's fucking me with. When he pulls it away, I say, "No... please... more."

"Not tonight, Kitten."

But he does grant me another orgasm, this time with his fingers, still refusing to allow me the penetration I seek.

I feel weak and shaky when Seven takes me off the St. Andrew's Cross. He carries me to the bed and arranges us so that he sits against the headboard and I'm leaning back against his chest.

"Open your legs," he orders.

I spread my legs and Declan joins us with the wax and cloth strips. I know he can see the fear in my eyes.

"It's okay, Pretty Toy. I know what I'm doing."

Before he starts, though, he bends down and licks between my legs. I arch off the bed into his hungry mouth. He makes me come again while Seven holds me still for him.

When Declan finally starts waxing, I'm relieved to find that he does know what he's doing. The heated wax is somehow soothing and not too hot. And he knows just the right way to rub over the cloth. He gives a nice clean rip, and though it hurts, it's only for a second. But I cry out each time; I can't help it.

Seven distracts me, stroking my breasts in a way that is somehow more soothing than erotic. "You're doing great," he says.

When Declan is finally finished, and I'm once again smooth and bare for them, he rubs a cooling salve between my legs.

"I'm going to take her to bed," Seven says.

I'm grateful when he picks me up and carries me up the stairs. I lay my head against his shoulder. On the main level, he takes me to the kitchen and sits me down on a bar stool. We eat some leftover pizza from the fridge. I find myself unable to believe he eats pizza.

When we get to Seven's room, he orders me to join him in the shower, but he isn't there to get either himself or me clean. And he's not there to fuck me, either. He holds my gaze while he takes my hand and wraps it around his cock.

I jerk him off in the shower.

"Fuck, yes. Just like that."

It only takes a few minutes before he comes over my hand. He leans forward, his head resting against my shoulder in an oddly sweet moment as he struggles to gain control of his breathing again.

He shuts the shower off, dries us both, then carries me to his bed. There are blackout shades in his room, and his balcony door is solid, not glass. He pulls the shades and turns out the light before joining me.

My breath hitches in my throat alone in the dark with him just as I've been so many nights before. I'm so sore and tender from where they waxed me. Even so, I would give almost anything for him to fuck me right now, even if it hurt. I'd pay that price just to feel him inside.

My legs fall open for him automatically, and he touches me like he always does in the dark. Except this time he's more careful than normal, slower and more gentle. He uses lube to stroke me, and I come apart under his hands.

Even after I've come, I want to ask for more, but I don't. He presses a kiss to my forehead.

"Sleep, Kitten."

12

W e have a late breakfast, this time in the kitchen. Part of me thought since I'm their slave, and they can do whatever they want with me, that I would start taking over domestic duties. Even if they have a cleaning service, maybe they don't have a cook. But they seem to be content doing the cooking themselves.

I've been allowed clothing today—jeans and a pale pink tank top. In fact, I was shocked to find my closet and drawers filled with clothes and shoes and undergarments all in my sizes. I suppose if they were planning this for a long time, they had plenty of time to get clothes for me.

Declan and Seven are both dressed sharply in suits, and it occurs to me I have no idea what they even do with their lives. I know Seven at least has always been well off, but what do they actually *do* during the day now that their life is back to the status quo? I don't bother asking because I'm sure they'll tell me it's none of my business, and I'm not sure I want to know the way men without conscience manage to acquire this much wealth and power over the police force.

Seven glances down at his watch. "Eleven a.m., Kitten. You're off the leash. See you at six. Each of them kiss me as though we are in some sort of unconventional, yet still fairly normal relationship. Then they just... leave. The house.

I stare after them, gaping like a fish. When I'm able to snap out of this fugue state, I step outside the main door to find that yes, they're driving off the property in separate cars. I find my blue Porsche sitting shiny and gleaming in the circular driveway. I have no idea how it got here, and it looks like someone washed it.

A young man who I hadn't noticed before, hands me the keys. "The car is ready, Ms. Mitchell. Mr. Kelly said to take care of it for you." He speaks in good but slightly broken English. His accent is unmistakable, but I can't fully place its origin.

"What about the gate?" I find myself asking.

"There's a programmed remote in the glove box." He opens the passenger side and shows me a slim black remote control with a single button.

"Thanks," I manage. My fingers drift unconsciously up to touch my collar. With the pink gemstones, it looks like regular jewelry, especially since it matches what I'm wearing, but still, I feel exposed. I also feel a bit like a puppy with a shock collar to keep me from straying too far.

They must feel very confident in their powers to keep me while giving me the illusion of freedom.

I put the keys in my pocket and take a walk around the

property. There are a few gardeners in the gardens. There's an enormous pool on one side of the house with what I would consider a "party jacuzzi". It's all decked out on the far end of the house for BBQs as though this is an activity Seven and Declan engage in routinely. I just can't see it.

When I make my way back around to the front of the house, there are several white vans parked in the drive.

The guy who washed my car notices my wariness and says, "It's just the cleaning service, Ms. Mitchell."

I manage a weak smile. Then I go inside and as unobtrusively as possible do a walk-through of the house. It's just beginning to dawn on me that I *live* here now. The penthouse was swank, no question, but this is on another level.

For all my ambition when I worked at the ad agency and the level of success I'd acquired, I'd never thought of myself as materialistic. Aside from the Louis Vuitton bag, I didn't put a lot of stock in things. And they didn't impress me. My drive for success was more about the pleasure of being the best at something and less about the financial rewards even though I *did* enjoy them.

But I can't help but stand in absolute awe of this exquisite house. There's a huge formal dining room on the first floor just off the generous entryway. There's a sort of fancy game room with billiard tables. There is literally a room which I think is meant just for smoking cigars and drinking whatever manly drink men prefer to have with cigars.

There is a solarium and an indoor pool. A library that extends up two stories. A fitness room. A fucking ballroom. Is there any reason to ever leave a house like this and go out into the world? I half expect to come across a restaurant or a gift shop, but of course I don't. There are a few smaller, cozier rooms that most people would call things like "living room". At the end of the hallway is a nice large office, but when I push the door open to one, a maid says, "I wouldn't, Ms. Mitchell, that's Mr. Kelly's private office."

I'm a bit troubled that I don't know which one of my masters Mr. Kelly is. I think it's probably Seven, but I don't know for sure, and I feel confident Seven and Declan won't submit to an interrogation about the matter, so I quietly shut the door.

"Sorry, I was just exploring."

She smiles, not unkindly, and goes on about her business.

I'm also a little weirded out that every single bit of staff knows my name. The second floor has several large nice bedrooms with balconies, several of which have their own bathrooms, like mine. None of the rooms are Declan's or Seven's. It's the third floor where I find their rooms. They look different in the day. Both are understated and masculine.

Having seen just about everything there is to see, I go back outside and get in my car. I don't remember the way here, so I program the address of my penthouse into the GPS.

It only takes about thirty minutes to get back to the city. It seemed farther away, but I guess every drive feels long when you're drunk, scared, and about to lose all your freedom to people you know you can't truly trust.

I go back to my penthouse and just sit on the sofa, staring out at the view of the city. I'm still processing all of this. I order in pizza and watch TV and take a bubble bath trying to feel normal. I'm still not sure if that drunk phone call was my worst idea or my best.

I get back home ten minutes before six to find Seven standing in the main entryway, still wearing the suit. My mouth goes dry. That look really works for him. "We're having dinner in the formal dining room. I'm told you've snooped around so you know where it is."

I'm not sure if he's upset about that. They didn't say I couldn't look around. They never said any area of the house was off limits.

"I'm sorry, Master," I say even though I don't really feel I owe him an apology.

He smirks. "For knowing where the dining room is? Yes, you should surely be punished for that high crime. Go upstairs. There's a dress for you on the bed. Put it on and come down. Dinner's almost ready."

Upstairs, draped across the bed is the most sophisticated black evening gown I've ever seen, and a pair of silver heels. I dress and fix my hair and makeup then stand for a few minutes admiring myself in the leaner mirror. The pink gemstones glitter in the light. The band isn't too thick and clunky, so it doesn't seem out of place.

"You really are a pretty toy."

I spin around to find Declan—also still in a suit—leaning against the door frame.

"Dinner's ready; come down now."

"Yes, Master," I say, but he's already disappeared down the hallway.

I move slower than him in heels, so I never quite catch up. When I reach the formal dining room, fine bone china and crystal has been laid out. The silverware is actual silver. Servants are serving some type of soup in shallow elegant bowls.

Seven sits at the head of the table. Declan is seated to his right. There's another place setting across from Declan. One of the servants pulls out that chair for me, and I sit.

"You look beautiful, Kitten," Seven says.

"Thank you."

"I'm sorry, what?"

"Thank you, Sir," I attempt, hoping he'll take that because we aren't alone in this room.

"No," he says flatly, even as his hazel eyes flash with emotion. "That will not work for me. Try again, Kitten."

"Thank you, Master," I murmur as I feel the flush crawl over my skin.

"Good girl."

We've just finished dinner in the formal dining room when the doorbell rings. Seven and Declan remain seated. I hear the front door open, some murmured words, and then a moment later a dangerous-looking man with dark hair and coal black eyes steps into the room. He, too, wears a suit, but even dressed nice, he looks rough and hardened, which makes the suit seem ill-fitted, even though it's as well-tailored as Seven's and Declan's.

I tense as his gaze sweeps appreciatively over me. There's something slimy and oily about the way he looks at me. He lingers on my cleavage before moving up, but not to my face. To my collar.

He knows. Then he looks me straight in the eyes and smiles.

His attention shifts to Seven.

"I thought I'd never get a meeting. I heard you were gone for a few weeks."

Seven's gaze cuts to me for the barest second, then back to his visitor. He seems unruffled by the man standing in the dining room.

"International business. It couldn't be helped. You could always have met with Declan. I've been back for a while, but I've been busy."

I realize this *international business* was when he was in the cell with me, playing his game while Declan handled all his outside affairs.

"I didn't want Declan. I wanted you," he says.

Declan pretends to be offended by this, but I know he doesn't care.

The stranger's attention shifts back to me again. "I see you have a new pet. I know you'll want to share her. Same price as always?" He comes around the table, and stands behind me.

I squeeze my eyes shut as his fingertips brush against my throat. I want to beg. I'm not even opposed to calling him master right now, even with an audience because this man knows anyway, and I'll do anything to keep his hands off me, but I'm too afraid to beg. It could make Seven look weak. And I know he'd never forgive that.

"Do. Not. Touch. Her." Seven says. His voice is cold and boiling all at once, both dead and the most alive he's ever been.

Declan stands, his hand going to his waist, and I realize suddenly he has a gun.

The stranger immediately pulls his hand back, and I let out a relieved sigh.

"You usually share."

"Not this one," Seven says.

"What's so special about her?" he asks, still pushing.

"Do you want to walk out of this room tonight?" Seven challenges.

The man's tone shifts sharply as he becomes aware of the threat and finally reads the room properly. "Yes, Mr. Kelly. I apologize. I won't ask again."

"Good. Spread the word. No one asks. Ever."

"Yes, Mr. Kelly. Of course."

Seven drops his napkin on his plate and stands. "Let's go to my study and talk business."

The stranger leaves the dining room, followed by Seven. Declan rises also.

"Go to your room and wait for us, Pretty Toy." He gives me a once-over. "And don't take the dress off."

It's a while before Seven and Declan come to my room. I worry briefly that something bad happened, that one or both of them is hurt, or worse. But of course this is silly. The house has too much electronic security. Besides, there are other people here tonight. And Declan, at least, is armed. Maybe Seven, too.

Seven is already loosening his tie when he steps into the room. His intense predatory gaze locks on mine, and for a moment, I think he's angry with me.

I'm standing. Declan said to leave the dress on, and I can't kneel in it. It's too tight in the wrong places. Plus, it's silk. I don't want to damage it.

They prowl around me, taking a good look at the dress. Then both of them are running their hands over my body encased in this exquisite fabric. Finally, they stop circling me like I'm prey. Declan is in front and Seven at my back. They begin to kiss my exposed skin as Seven pulls down the zipper of the gown. They work together undressing me.

I'm surprised when Seven is tying a blindfold around my eyes. Then one of them takes my hands in his.

"I'm taking your ass tonight," Seven growls in my ear. Besides punishing me, this is the other thing he wasn't able to do while he was getting the thrill of pretending to be my protector. And I find myself wanting it as much as he does.

"Thank you, Master." These words just come to me, and I say them because I know he'll get off on it.

He chuckles. "We trained you so well. Such a natural. I knew when I first saw you the day we started watching you that you were the one for us."

In other circumstances, some of those words might have passed for romantic.

Both men help me onto the bed. Declan guides me to straddle him. I know which of them is which by the way they touch me. I'm already wet, so hungry for the fucking I've been denied since my return as if I were being punished for playing their game the way they designed it.

He lets out a hiss of pleasure as I lower myself onto him. A mouth latches onto my breast and I know from the angles, that it's Declan's. He bites my nipple hard enough to elicit a cry from me, and his answering chuckle reverberates against my skin.

Seven is busy placing open-mouthed kisses against my throat. I'm still adjusting to Declan inside me. I'd forgotten how big he was. My body has had too much rest from them.

"Fuck me," Declan orders.

I begin to move.

Seven is kissing my back, pressing a kiss against the small of it—something I had thought was only a Declan thing. I like it. It's strangely tender and intimate. A drawer opens and closes. And then a lubed toy is being worked inside my ass. Tears stream down my face. Not pain—relief that this is finally happening again.

"Shhhh, Kitten," Seven says, misunderstanding the cause of my tears. He strokes my back as the toy slides in and out of me. Declan's fingers dig into my hips arching and thrusting upward.

Then the toy is gone, and it's Seven. I gasp when he pushes himself inside me. He grabs my throat and pulls me back against him. His mouth is at my ear.

"This is the best place my dick has ever been," he growls, which sends another jolt of arousal between my legs.

One of Declan's hands leaves my hip as his thumb moves against my clit. I'm lost in a sea of darkness behind the blindfold unable to do anything but feel them both as they fill me, stretching me, claiming me in the most complete and carnal way I've ever experienced.

Now that the mask is off, Seven is the rougher lover. But the force with which he takes me only drives me higher and faster toward my peak.

Then, in the most unlikely of sexual lotteries, all three of us come at the same time. We are a symphonic mix of my whimpers and their animalistic growls. Seven pulls out of me, pushing me forward over Declan, spilling himself onto my back as my pussy clenches around and milks the rest of Declan's release, greedily sucking it inside me.

I rise off of Declan. He removes the blindfold and pulls me down to lie against his chest, stroking my hair. I expect that now all three of us will cuddle together in this bed. It feels like what should come next. But it isn't what comes next.

"You can have her in your bed tonight," Seven says, getting dressed. Then he leaves the room without another word.

I stare after him, wondering if I've done something wrong, wondering if now that he's scratched these twin itches of punishment and fucking my ass if he finds it wasn't truly worth the wait after all. Is he bored now? Declan notices my distress.

"It's not you, Kate. He's got some business to take care of. It's fine."

I nod, not feeling reassured.

Declan doesn't fuck me again tonight. Instead, he takes me up to his room on the third floor and pulls me into the shower with him. He silently washes me, and I wash him. It's intimate, but not sexual in the way one would expect. Then we lie down together in his bed. He pulls me into him—always and forever his little spoon. It's the first time I'm able to fully relax into this moment where we are wrapped in a tender embrace inside his bed. It's the first time I don't warn myself that it isn't real.

13

Months go by in this new normal. Declan was right, it wasn't me. Seven grows distant at times, but he always comes back to me, giving me that glimmer of the man I first knew.

Each morning passes much as any ordinary couple might pass it—except that it's three instead of two. Every day we have breakfast in a strangely comfortable silence at the kitchen table, they kiss me, and they leave. Then I go about my day.

I've gotten to know the names of most of the staff as they come and go. I still don't know what Seven and Declan do, though I'm certain it's some kind of organized crime. On the second day of our new arrangement, I learned they have security that goes well beyond electronic. Guards. And it's really a full-on security team. No wonder they weren't afraid I'd ask the staff for help. The guards stay outside and work in shifts. There are two security buildings, one at the front near the gate and one at the back end of the property.

That, combined with the occasional unsavory visitors who come to the house, retreating always to a private study to talk business with Seven, and it's not as though I need a diagram. Many of these men look at me with clear lust in their gaze, knowing exactly what I am to my masters, and also knowing they will never be allowed to touch me no matter what they did with *the others*.

I wonder what happened to the others? And did Seven and Declan start with the same game they did with me? Or did they go a different route? Did they use their money from the very beginning to simply buy what they wanted? Did they want my submission to come from a different place? After all, when they first offered me my freedom, I only took it because it seemed I didn't have the option to stay. And when I came back, I thought I was going back to the cell. So it wasn't for their money.

For the first few weeks, I used my *outdoor kitty* time to shop and take in some movies, and of course, the spa. But it got boring. I missed work. So I started working on setting up my own ad agency.

It's not a traditional agency. I don't have the necessary freedom to do that. I redid the penthouse to function as a place to meet clients. I'll only take a few at a time, and my availability is by appointment only. But it seems to be working out.

When I get home in the evenings, we eat. I've since learned that actually they do have a cook who comes in several days a week to prepare meals. Though they also like to cook part of the time and always for breakfast.

After dinner, things stop being quite so benign. They torment me endlessly with pleasure while demanding the same from me along with my absolute obedience. They use me in whatever way pleases them, but no matter what they do, my body always hungers for more. Sometimes I sleep in my own bed, but more often than not, I'm invited into either Declan's or Seven's bed for the night.

I look down at my phone to check the time and am filled with horror. It's almost six. I've never been late coming home. Will they think I ran? Will they come after me? I'm so scared of how they might punish me for this infraction that I can't think straight. I've come to trust over time that as fucked-up as they are, they really do seem to feel something for me and to not want to cause me actual harm.

At the same time, that doesn't stop the fact that they are terrifying, and I've disobeyed their orders. I try to think of an appropriate lie, even though I know I'm not a good liar and that will probably only make things worse.

Hell, maybe I should wreck the car so I have an excuse. The fact that I'm even thinking such crazy thoughts is a testament to how wrong I am now. I'm so... *wrong*. But if they took the collar off my throat and told me to leave, I would beg them to let me stay. There's no saving me anymore. My body, mind, and soul, have long been theirs.

And when I don't judge myself or think about how society would feel about this, how they might judge or pity me, I think I'm actually happy. But if I'm so happy, why am I so scared to go home so late?

Aside from what they've done to twist my mind, they truly have never harmed me. They've never lost their tempers with me. The only reason I've ever felt my life was in danger at their hands was because of what I know about their lack of remorse. They don't have the same leash on them that other people have.

It's not so much that they're evil—at least not to me— it's that they're wild. They're like wild animals. You can work with a wild predatory animal every day for years... You can believe you've built trust, that the animal sees you as a friend. And then one day, out of nowhere, the tiger mauls you to death. This is what I worry about. That they'll get bored with me, and that one day that switch inside them will flip, and their predatory gaze will settle on me, and my number's up.

But I'm too fucked-up now to live outside their cage. I tried. I do believe they care for me, probably more than they've ever cared for anything besides each other. But am I fooling myself? Is it a false sense of security that every time I walk inside the tiger's cage, I'm certain I'm getting out alive?

Yet I'm sure I'm the equivalent of the serial killer's wife of two decades. He will never ever harm her. He will wear that mask and make her feel loved, and maybe she's the one person who can make him feel anything. I like that feeling. Being that one person that someone cares about. There's no other human being who can turn their gaze or hold their attention, and there's a rush of power in that which I'm ashamed I like.

Even if they ever let me go, even if I somehow could go on without them, I would be lonely for the rest of my life. They have ruined me for any other relationship, no matter how healthy and good and true it might be. I've become twisted in the tangled vines of their darkness, and there's nowhere left to go but down.

Maybe I should call and apologize, explain to them that I just lost track of time. I left my cell phone in the car and wonder if they've already tried to call or text. My hands shake as I fumble with the key fob to get into the Porsche. I stumble back as a hand with a foul smelling cloth goes over my mouth.

WHEN I COME TO, A BLINDFOLD COVERS MY EYES, AND MY hands are tied together over my head. I'm still wearing my sundress, but my shoes are gone. My bare feet are cold under the hard floor. I still feel foggy from the drugs. Why the fuck did they drug me? Did they really think that was necessary?

"Please... I'm sorry..." I whimper. The tears are already rolling down my cheeks. "I... I lost track of the time... please forgive me, Master."

A hand grips my throat, hard. Harder than normal. I gasp and choke for air, struggling against the ropes.

A laugh. "Master? My, what fucked-up games has my frigid little bitch been playing?"

My heart sinks. Andrew.

"You LIED to me," he hisses in my ear as he rips off the blindfold.

I look frantically around. We're in an abandoned meat-packing plant. The ropes tied around my wrists are looped up over a hook that once held dead animal carcasses.

"You were never going to be homeless. You tricked me

into caring again and coming to your rescue, and you were gone. Why didn't you answer my calls and messages? WHY? Too busy laughing with a new lover? You obviously found someone very well off with that car you're driving," he sneers.

He looks crazed. I have no idea what to say to him. He won't believe me if I tell him I was kidnapped. What kind of kidnapper lets their victim go and furnishes them with a Porsche? I'm still trying to process the fact that I'm not tied up for punishment from my masters but for some kind of revenge from my ex-boyfriend.

It sickens me to think I voluntarily dated this piece of shit for as long as I did. He was a mean asshole and bad in bed, but I didn't think he was a violent criminal. I hold onto the small thread of hope that he's bluffing or can't bring himself to do whatever it is he's psyching himself up to do.

"Andrew, this is crazy. It's not what you think. You need to untie me." It takes everything in me not to say the word Master again. Not because I would ever think of Andrew in that way but because I've been so conditioned these past few months to respond with that word when afraid, when tied up, when at someone else's mercy.

And then I see the knife, and the real panic begins.

"Andrew... please."

"Andrew, please," he mimics in a high voice. "This is the only way you'll learn not to be such a lying fucking bitch." He slices my sundress in several places and rips it off me. Then he does the same with my panties. I'm not wearing a bra for him to destroy.

He goes for my collar, fumbling for a clasp or way to get it off. "Why won't this come off? Why is it locked on?"

The collar. It's become so much a part of me that I forget it's there half the time. I silently pray Seven and Declan are on their way. But how long will they wait before thinking I've tried to run and come for me? And how do I even know there's really a tracking device inside? How would a tracking device be inside?

The tears slide down my cheeks as I realize it was probably just another mindfuck—just something to scare me, to train me and make me obey. What if there isn't a tracking device? And even if there is, what if they haven't gotten concerned enough about my absence to bother coming after me? I could be dead long before they even leave the house.

Andrew takes a step back and stares at the collar, then back at me, then at the collar again, then back at me as he finally puts two and two together.

"Oh. My. God. You fucking whore. This is delicious. I'd fuck you before I killed you, but we both know you'll be dry, you frigid fucking bitch. How on earth did you get some man to play kinky sex games with you when you can't even come? Does he just keep you around for blow jobs? I recall you're actually talented there. Maybe I'll let you blow me before I cut you up."

I'm crying seriously now—not just a few delicate tears sliding down my cheeks but full-on sobbing. I no longer have just basic fear of punishment for getting home late, but terror as the reality of who has me and why he's taken me has finally clicked inside my drug-addled brain.

"Andrew, please... please, I'm sorry, please... don't hurt me."

I want to spit in his face. I want to swing back and kick out at him. But I want to live more. I want to see Seven and Declan again. I want to be back home with them. I rack my brain, trying to figure out how to calm him down and somehow get out of this.

I flinch and try to pull away as he presses the tip of the knife at my throat and slowly drags it downward, not drawing blood, not yet. He wants me as afraid as I can possibly be. Maybe he's bluffing. Maybe he just wants to scare me. I hold onto this thought because I still just can't believe he's a killer. I can't believe he would cut me.

"Y-you don't want to do this. I'm not worth prison."

He laughs again. "Trust me, baby, I won't get caught." He makes a small, shallow cut across my collar bone, his eyes lighting with delighted malice at the sight of my blood.

I yelp at the thin burning streak. Then my gaze shifts as I catch movement in the shadows. It's them.

I catch Seven's eye. "Master, please..."

"I'm not your *Master*," Andrew says. "You're not worth that much investment, you little freak."

A throat clears, and Andrew nearly jumps out of his skin as he realizes we aren't alone.

"I believe she was referring to me," Seven says, stepping out of the shadows.

Andrew turns wildly, this time holding the knife up like he thinks he's going to fight him with it.

Declan joins Seven, and the two of them throw the full force of their dark, blank stares on Andrew. They are terrifying when they drop the masks and let that cold, menacing darkness swirl out of them.

"Andrew, Andrew, Andrew," Seven says. "This is awkward. We were grateful that you practically gift-wrapped a girl with nothing to lose and nowhere to go for us to just pick right up. But she doesn't belong to you, pal. She belongs to us, and I'm afraid touching our toys is a killing offense."

"Indeed," Declan says.

They are both so calm, and I swear it's a thousand times more frightening than the erratic insanity that just came out of Andrew.

"Drop the knife and step away from our girl," Declan says.

Instead, Andrew moves behind me, pressing the tip of the blade to my throat. "I'll kill her."

Seven laughs. "And what will that get you? Longer torture, probably. Kill her, don't kill her. Either way, you're ours now. And we aren't nearly so gentle with men."

Andrew presses the blade harder against my skin. I cry as another small trickle of blood flows out.

"Master... please."

Neither Seven nor Declan flinches. Nothing changes on their impassible faces. Both men charge so fast toward Andrew, that he actually takes a step back and drops the knife. I can't see what happens behind me, but I hear the scuffling, Andrew's yelping, some punching.

They drag him around in front of me, forcing him to his knees. Declan holds the knife at his throat.

"Beg for forgiveness," Declan says.

"P-please, I'm sorry. Please forgive me. D-don't let them kill me," Andrew sputters.

Seven hauls him off the ground. "That's fucking pathetic. We don't need to hear any more of *that*. And *let* us kill you? Please."

Seven holds him while Declan takes out a coil of rope from his inside jacket pocket. He ties the ropes so hard and violently I flinch. They hang him from a meat hook so that he's facing me.

The two men take a couple of steps back. They look back and forth from Andrew to me. Aren't they going to untie me and let me down? It hurts that they acted like they didn't care if Andrew killed me. I know if they'd shown that weakness or hesitation that I'd be in more danger, but it still hurts because a part of me is scared that was the truth—that I'm only a toy to them, only a pet, and they would be barely bothered if I died.

"Now, Andrew," Seven says, but he's circling and looking at me. "Let's talk about this frigid bitch comment."

Declan moves up behind me, his mouth peppering kisses across my throat as his tongue slips out and licks the spot on my neck where Andrew pressed the blade.

I can't stop the small whimper as my fear shifts to arousal. I'm sure most people couldn't make such a swift mental shift, but I've been making that shift for so long now that it feels like my default factory setting. Suddenly, the adrenaline inside me has a safe place to land.

"Who do you belong to?" Seven asks.

"You and Declan, Master."

Declan's hands have snaked around to begin to rub my breasts. I arch shamelessly into his touch. I know this is sick and twisted, but my head falls back against his shoulder, and I close my eyes, letting him fondle me however he wants.

I jump at a hard slap. But there's no pain because I wasn't the recipient. Seven just slapped Andrew.

"Keep your eyes open. Watch. Her. Before you die, you need to know that she was always perfect. The problem was always you. You are the failure. You are the one who doesn't know how to touch a woman and keep her happy. You destroyed her life because you are a fuck up. Watch how responsive she is. Look at what you could have had, you fucking fool."

There is malice in Andrew's gaze as it meets mine. And the part of me that my masters have twisted beyond repair loves it because there isn't a goddamn thing he can do to me now. It hurt every time he called me frigid, every time he acted as though there was something wrong and broken with me that I couldn't come with him. And I don't just mean on the inside, I mean at all. I couldn't come at all with him. And now he's getting a front row seat to the truth and what he could never have.

Maybe it should bother me more that he's watching this, but he's seen me naked hundreds of times. He's never seen this, though.

"You will not say a single word while this is happening," Seven tells Andrew. "Otherwise, we'll keep you alive longer, and trust me when I say you don't want that."

Declan strokes between my legs, pushing two large fingers inside me. He rubs my inner walls, knowing exactly how and where to touch me. And then Seven joins him, and he kisses me, his hand gripped possessively around my neck while Declan continues his relentless finger fucking. It doesn't take long for me to come. They've trained me too well. Seven pulls back to allow my screams of pleasure to fill the abandoned factory.

Declan doesn't stop until I beg him, pleading that I can't take anymore.

"What do you say to me?" he asks, still gently fondling me, not ready to stop yet.

"Thank you, Master," I say on a sated sigh. I give him this without shame or fear. He pulls his hand away, pressing his wet fingers into my mouth. I suck on them without prompting.

"Such a good girl," he soothes, stroking my hair.

I can only whimper in reply.

When I come down off this high, I open my eyes and look over at Andrew. I expect to see shock or disgust on his face. But instead, I see raw lust and anger, as though I had been somehow selfishly withholding this from him all this time.

My gaze shifts to Seven. He's standing next to Andrew again, but he's watching me.

"Take her to the car," Seven says.

Declan lifts the ropes binding my arms off the hook. I'd lost track of how much that hurt, hanging there, but now I'm newly aware. He unties the ropes and rubs my wrists, then he brings each one to his lips, kissing the chafed skin. He lifts me up and carries me out of the factory. The sun has disappeared behind the trees, and I shiver against the chill in the air.

He settles me in the car and takes off his suit jacket and puts it on me. He takes a first aid kit out of the glove box and rubs an aloe gel into my wrists where the ropes rubbed me raw in my struggle.

Classical music flows into the car as he turns the key in the ignition. He turns the heat on.

"Stay," he orders.

I nod. Why would I run now?

14

I watch the clock on the dash as it marches on. Two hours pass before Declan returns to the car. In the glare of the headlights I can see his shirt is covered in blood. I'm surprisingly horrified by this. I knew they were monsters. But I've never seen it in this visceral, violent way before. He and Seven just spent all this time torturing a man to death while I sat out in the car in the dark. This is what they have inside them.

As bad as Andrew was, it still twists something in my gut to know the amount of suffering he just endured. It's so stupid because he had every intention to carve me up like a turkey. Declan takes off the bloody shirt, pops the trunk, and stuffs it inside before getting into the driver's side.

He starts to pull out of the huge parking lot.

"Wait... what about Seven?"

"He's doing clean up and disposal. He'll meet us back at the house later."

I almost ask how the hell he'll do that if we take the car

but then I realize he's going to take Andrew's car... and get rid of it.

We drive silently away from the meat-packing plant and onto a lonely abandoned road. I'm lost deep in thought. I was with Andrew for two years. I thought he was an asshole, a piece of shit. Was he also a sociopath? It's so tempting to try to shift him into that category. He was going to torture me to death. I have no doubt of that.

We want to believe every violent terrible person is *crazy*. We want to believe every sociopath is a crazed violent lunatic. But I'm not sure if that's true. We want to believe that there's a special category of not-really-human who does bad things and that we can never be in that category because we're sane. We're real people, and they are not.

But just being with Seven and Declan, I've felt pieces of my humanity shut off. I find myself influenced by the way they see the world around them. And what just happened back there... me happily letting them get me off while Andrew watched... something is definitely broken and changed in me. But I'm not a monster.

I know now that Andrew is a monster. But is Andrew empty in the way Seven and Declan are? The idea that I could be safe with the men I'm with but in danger from someone who has no actual mental illness is unsettling.

While I'm thinking all this, I'm very aware that Seven is happily chopping up a body to dispose of. And I'm sure he's happy about it. Possibly gleeful.

In college I took sociology because I thought it would help me in the advertising world. Psychology is the normal choice, and there's a lot of overlap, but if you want to sell a lot of a product, you need to know how people act in herds, not just as individuals.

I remember an experiment we learned about called the Milgram experiment. It showed that normal, good, moral people in shockingly large numbers will obey an authority figure to act against their own conscience to harm a random innocent person. So I'm not sure I'm any more unsafe with these men than I would be with some "good" person.

At least every decision Seven and Declan make comes absolutely from their own will with no other influence. There's a strange safety in that. I stare out the window, clutching Declan's coat around me as I watch the trees move by in a blur outside the window. Night has settled in more deeply, growing comfortable in its cloak of darkness. The full moon rises over the treetops, and there's a strange peace in this moment.

"Are you all right?" he finally asks.

At least I don't have to make up an excuse for being home late. I can't believe that's the thought I'm thinking right now. What have these men done to my mind?

"Yes, Master. Thank you for coming to get me." I almost say thank you for putting the tracking device in my collar, but that's too crazy even for me. Absently, I trail my fingertips over the metal band around my throat that just saved my life.

When we get home, Declan takes me to the master bathroom attached to Seven's room. He runs a hot bath and lights some candles for me.

"Take a bath and then come downstairs. I'll make you something to eat."

"Thank you, Master."

He just nods and leaves. I take off the suit coat and lay it across the bed in Seven's room, then I turn off the bathroom lights so there's only the soft glow of the candles and get into the tub.

I think I was in shock back at the plant because I finally cry. I let all these feelings inside me come out... the latent fear over what could have so easily happened, and the relief that it didn't, the relief that I'm back home.

I soak for a very long time, but finally I get out of the bath and dry off, blowing out the candles on the way out of the room. I go to my room and find something to wear, selecting a white sundress with small yellow flowers on it. Declan and Seven both like this dress. I'm only allowed underwear when I have my time out of my cage each day so I don't put any on.

When I get downstairs, I find the kitchen table set for three. Declan has made homemade beef pot pie. It's a soothing, comforting meal and exactly what I need right now. He always knows exactly what I need.

The front door opens and slams shut, and a few minutes later, Seven stands in the kitchen doorway. He's covered in blood, much like Declan was, only worse because he had to actually cut up the body. I shudder at that thought.

His gaze finds mine. "Are you okay?"

"Yes, Master."

"How did it go?" Declan asks.

"No one will ever find him," Seven replies.

"And the car?"

"Same. I'm going to grab a quick shower." Seven disappears from the room as Declan pours some tea into my glass and puts a generous serving of pot pie on my plate.

"Eat," he orders.

I thought we'd wait on Seven, but he doesn't have to tell me twice. I'm so hungry. Every few bites I look up to find his gray gaze on me. He's eating, too, but he doesn't take his eyes from mine. He doesn't say anything.

Is he trying to figure out if I'm really okay? If any lasting psychological damage was done? Part of me thinks they would have enjoyed torturing the life from Andrew even if he'd done nothing wrong just for the sheer sport of it. It's convenient that there was a justifiable excuse.

Fifteen minutes later, Seven is back downstairs, wearing only jeans, water dripping down his back from his still wet hair. He sits across from me and digs in, eating like this is the first meal he's had in a week. He doesn't look up at me until he's cleaned his plate.

"Do you want more?" Declan asks me, noticing my plate is clean, too.

"No, Master."

He nods and clears all of our plates from the table.

"Go up to my room and wait for us," Seven says.

A shiver skates down my spine at this command.

When I get to Seven's room, I strip off the dress and get into his huge bed. When they join me, I don't get the rough claiming fucking I expected. I assumed they would want to piss on their territory. After another man had his hands on me—even if the situation wasn't my choice—surely they'd want to fuck me in a way so there was no mistake who I belonged to, lest any creature with breath in its lungs forget.

But they don't do this. Instead, they are so careful, gentle as though I might break. Soft kisses, gentle caresses, murmured endearments I no longer know if I should let myself believe, yet can't chastise myself for hoping are real. They don't fuck me together. They take turns, and each of them is slow and deliberate, savoring the feel of their body inside of mine.

My monsters take such very good care of me. Maybe they can't really feel love, but I've heard that the early kind of love in a relationship is only infatuation, that it isn't real. Everyone who claims to really know says that love isn't a feeling; it's an action.

If love is an action, then my monsters definitely love me. Maybe they can't feel the same things other people can feel, but they do take care of me. And they do want me.

I don't know if they're still playing a game with me or if what we have is real, but either way, I'll play.